# A Candlelight Ecstasy Romance ®

## "DO YOU THINK YOU CAN GET AWAY? DO YOU THINK I'LL LET YOU?"

The kiss went deeper, searching the shape of her lips as they warmed to his. The stern seriousness of his eyes, the hand still behind her neck, gentle but firm, the fact that he'd kissed her before without things getting out of control, and an inexplicable need for him, all combined to make her tilt her mouth upward and slowly close her eyes. His arms enfolded her, cradled her lovingly. Yet she could sense the strength of his passion boiling just beneath the surface, felt him controlling it as his mouth feasted hungrily on hers.

## A CANDLELIGHT ECSTASY ROMANCE ®

# DESIRE AND CONQUER

*Diane Dunaway*

*A CANDLELIGHT ECSTASY ROMANCE* ®

Published by
Dell Publishing Co., Inc.
1 Dag Hammarskjold Plaza
New York, New York 10017

Dell ® TM 681510, Dell Publishing Co., Inc.

Candlelight Ecstasy Romance®, 1,203,540,
is a registered trademark of Dell Publishing
Co., Inc., New York, New York.

ISBN: 0–440–11779–8

Printed in the United States of America
First printing—July 1983

*To the loving memory of Fernella,
a brilliant and courageous Arabian mare,
and all the miles we traveled*

To Our Readers:

We have been delighted with your enthusiastic response to Candlelight Ecstasy Romances®, and we thank you for the interest you have shown in this exciting series.

In the upcoming months we will continue to present the distinctive, sensuous love stories you have come to expect only from Ecstasy. We look forward to bringing you many more books from your favorite authors and also the very finest work from new authors of contemporary romantic fiction.

As always, we are striving to present the unique absorbing love stories that you enjoy most—books that are more than ordinary romance.

Your suggestions and comments are always welcome. Please write to us at the address below.

Sincerely,

The Editors
Candlelight Romances
1 Dag Hammarskjold Plaza
New York, New York 10017

# CHAPTER ONE

"And the next and last contestant in our jumping class this afternoon is number one hundred and one, Desert King, ridden by Jennifer Globe and owned by Globe Enterprises," the announcer's voice said clearly over the loudspeaker.

It was the Santa Barbara All-Arabian Horse Show, the biggest show of the season, and Jennifer Globe had never been so nervous.

The twelve other contestants in the jumping class had already ridden over the course of eight jumps set up around the white-railed arena. And it was her turn next. If her horse jumped all eight fences without a fault, and in less than fifty-two seconds, she would win. Otherwise she would lose not only this class but her dream of being allowed to compete in the National Championships the following month.

Jennifer's gloved hand reached to pull her black velvet jumping hat lower over her eyes, checked to see that the first button on her red jumping coat was buttoned, and straightened her cravat, making sure the gold pin holding it was secure. Then the gate swung open and, taking a deep breath and slowly expelling it, she guided King into the ring.

Jennifer didn't even glance up at the boxes and the fifty tiers of seating around the arena or notice that they were filled to capacity and that every eye was on her. Her attention was given only to her horse and the course she must complete.

She leaned forward slightly, letting King break into a canter, feeling the eager strength of his warm body between her legs as she made one small circle, then a second. Then—as she said a silent prayer—with a touch of her spurless heel, Desert King was charging forward to the first jump—and to victory or defeat.

Rain the night before had made the arena muddy and slippery, but Jennifer didn't let herself think of the danger. Squaring her jaw, she leaned low in the saddle, urging King to go faster and balancing with her knees as he gathered himself and sprang into the air like a soaring black eagle.

He slipped as he landed and the audience gasped and held its breath as the sleek black animal almost went to his knees. But Jennifer kept her eyes fixed straight ahead, never losing her composure as King recovered and she headed him toward the next jump.

She rode like a fury, and the spectators, perched on the edges of their seats, neither moved nor spoke as she cleared the next seven obstacles at racing speed and crossed the finish line, where the judge pressed the stem of his stop watch and studied it intently before announcing, "Fifty-one seconds flat."

The applause was thunderous.

"That's my niece Jennifer," Walter Globe said to Flint Michaels, a long-time business associate he had invited to attend the show and share his private box.

Flint Michaels' dark green eyes followed the girl out of the arena. Then he answered, "You must be proud of her. She makes it look easy."

"Yes, Jennifer has won a houseful of trophies. Been showing for sixteen years, since she was nine. I thought she might quit when she went to college. But she gave up a scholarship to Stanford to stay at school at U.C. Santa

Barbara so she could be close by and manage the ranch. All these people"—he indicated the audience around them with a wave of his hand—"are crazy about Arabian horses and spend thousands of dollars a year to own them, breed them, and compete in horse shows that determine who has bred the finest." Walter Globe sipped his Scotch. "They've never been my hobby, but these people say Arabians are storybook horses like the kind you dreamed about having as a kid—a fantasy come true. I guess everyone loves fantasies. Take your business, for instance." Walter Globe indicated Flint with a lift of his glass. "You wouldn't have already made your third million before reaching thirty-five if people didn't love to pretend."

Flint laughed, his eyes crinkling at the corners, his white teeth visible in a handsome grin. "Yes, I guess you're right. The whole business venture started out as a fantasy, just a crazy idea some of us thought would work."

"A damned good idea too," Walter Globe added. "A damned creative idea, and a damned lucrative one. Who would have thought that so many people would want to put all those quarters in an electronic game called Space Wizard? I've got to hand it to you, Flint. You've certainly got good instincts. But that just proves my point. Everyone has to do something. You, for instance, have your Texas ranch and your business and all those beautiful women chasing you. Some people take up sailing or painting or playing your electronic games, while others, like these people, show their Arabians to keep from realizing how bored they really are."

The entries of the jumping class had been called back into the wide ring, and when they were lined up in the center facing the judges, the winner's number was announced and Jennifer rode forward to receive the blue ribbon and a silver cup, her bright smile visible beneath the velvet hat pulled low over her eyes..

11

"She's a lovely girl," Flint commented, not taking his eyes from her.

"Yes," Walter agreed. "I worry about her sometimes. Now that her parents are both dead she lives alone on the family ranch. I'm giving her a party there later tonight. Her aunt and I would be pleased if you'd come."

Flint nodded, his curious gaze still following Jennifer as she rode out the gate in triumph, the blue ribbon streaming from her gloved hand. "I'd like that," he said when she was out of sight. "I'd like that very much."

For the next few hours one class of beautiful Arabians followed another in and out of the ring while, with the flair of a host enjoying himself, Walter pointed out the favorites in each class, ordered drinks, told amusing anecdotes, and introduced Flint to his friends. Then, when it was over, they drove through the hills of Santa Barbara to Casa Contenta, the Globe family ranch, a rambling hacienda with numbers of Rolls-Royces and Ferraris already parked haphazardly in its front pasture.

Inside, champagne was flowing continuously from the spouts of a silver fountain set up in the center of the main room, and excusing himself from his other guests, Walter showed Flint around the two spacious floors.

A rock 'n' roll band was tuning up on the patio as Walter pointed out the many vine-covered balconies, the intricate wrought-iron grillwork, the rose garden off the presently unoccupied master bedroom. Then, pausing in the upstairs hall, a bit hazy from all the Scotch he had consumed, Walter confided that the hacienda, including its collection of Arabians, was for sale.

"Of course I think the horses are beautiful. But . . . well, Flint, actually Globe Enterprises is in trouble and although this ranch isn't losing money now, it is dead weight. I think it would be a sound investment in the hands of the right man, but I know nothing about horses, and while Jennifer has plans to make it profitable if Desert

King wins the championship, there are no guarantees. I hate to sell the ranch out from under her. She's lived here all her life and has a lot of pride in these animals. But with her reputation she could get top dollar for managing anyone's horses, and confidentially, Flint, Globe Enterprises needs cash. We just can't hang on much longer."

Flint, nodding with interest, was about to ask for details about the property when a high-pitched feminine voice interrupted them. "Flint Michaels, you devil! So here you are!" said the teasing, indignant voice that Flint recognized as Lillian Globe's even before she thrust herself into his arms and planted her lip-glossed mouth firmly on his.

He returned the kiss passionlessly before setting Lillian back on her spikey high heels. "Hello, Lillian," he said, casually running his eyes up and down the curves of her perfectly tanned body, enticingly displayed in the spaghetti-strapped red chiffon dress. "You're looking well."

Lillian slid an arm around his athletic waist, snuggling closer before looking up in her most appealing way. "I want you to know that tonight I'm not taking no for an answer. Last party Angela had you, but not tonight," she said, pressing her breast against his arm.

Flint smiled, his well-defined mouth parting to reveal a set of perfect teeth. It was an easy, natural expression. Nevertheless it conveyed a sense of power and virility that Lillian felt to the marrow of her bones. "Fine," he was saying, amused tolerance in his deep voice. "You have me. Now what?"

"Come on. Let's dance!" she said, already moving her body to the fast beat of the music. "Not now, Lillian," her father said, "Flint and I are talking business."

"Oh, business! This is a party! Anyway, if I'm going to be as successful as Flint I'm going to have to learn to take what I want like he does. And I want to dance."

"You'll excuse us," Flint said to Walter, who nodded reluctantly. "Maybe we'll talk again later."

13

Lillian headed for the dance floor and Flint followed to the center of the churning couples, where Lillian began a coordinated series of moves that invited much more than just dancing as her little tongue emerged occasionally to moisten her lips.

It was a long dance. Then the rock beat slowed and a black woman vocalist with a soft puff of black hair surrounding her face took the microphone and began a love ballad.

Immediately Lillian threw both arms around his neck and ground her hips sensuously into his. Then she kissed his ear and whispered, "I'm so sick of horses and horse showing and all these people, Flint. I don't understand *why* my father invited everyone here to a party for Jennifer when she doesn't even like parties." Lillian wrinkled her pretty nose. "Anyway, I think some of these people even smell like horses." She leaned closer, her tongue circling his earlobe. "It seems like I never see you alone anymore. Why don't we go upstairs? Jennifer is the only one who lives here now. She'll never know the difference if we use one of the guest rooms."

Flint was aware of his automatic male response to Lillian but this reaction didn't overcome the sense of growing boredom he experienced, not only with her but with most of the other women who regularly provided him with their company. It had been ten years now since an idea and some lucky investment capital had launched him into the glittering circle of the highly successful. Having grown up on a Texas ranch, he had found the wild parties, the abundance of beautiful women, the fawning attention, all part of an exciting new world. But recently the emptiness of this tinsel life had become more and more apparent, and the company of women like Lillian was beginning to seem like oatmeal—good only when he was either very cold or very hungry.

So, untangling himself by taking her two clinging hands

14

in his, Flint moved her to arm's length. "That's a nice offer, Lillian," he said with a remnant of a drawl, "but I'm not in the habit of making love with a woman right under her father's nose and particularly when he has a houseful of guests. The old-fashioned Texas code, I guess. We'll get together another time."

Lillian had experienced the firm hand before, the non-committal tone, the words that politely covered his rejection—and what irritated her most was the fact she had never been able to change his mind, once he had made it up. Still, she leaned forward, lifting her hands high to rest on his shoulders so that his gaze, tilted downward, could view her breasts, unemcumbered by a bra in the low-cut gown. "No—*now*, Flint! Can't you see I need you?"

It annoyed her to see there was no sign of passion in his eyes as he answered, "Lillian, it's only eight thirty. Be reasonable. Don't you think your father would miss us?"

"I don't care about my father—or any of his friends. Besides, what if they do know?"

A scattering of applause interrupted them and, following the direction of everyone's gaze, Flint found his eyes on a young woman who had just appeared at the top of the burnished wooden stairway that led across the room.

She was tall and slender; most of her height was in her long shapely legs. Her sculptured features were innocent of makeup and her long, sun-bleached blond hair was pulled straight back and clipped at the nape of her neck with a silver clasp that matched small hoop earrings in delicate pierced ears. Her silk dress was a deep aquamarine that matched her eyes and was straight-lined and belted at her unusually tiny waist.

She was beautiful, but there was something else besides her beauty—an intangible something very special about *this* woman, that made Flint lean and whisper to Lillian, "Who is that? Have I seen her before?"

Lillian snorted and gave a small dismissing wave of her

manicured hand. "My cousin Jennifer. You saw her this afternoon showing Desert King. That's why the applause. She must have won, I guess. I don't keep track. She's quiet and keeps to herself most the time. I don't blame you for not remembering her." Lillian gestured again, her long red finger nails flashing. "With her it's just horses and more horses and nothing else. I mean I think horses are pretty but I've found there are lots of *other* things in life." She snuggled into his shoulder.

Flint's green eyes fixed on Jennifer Globe and sparkled as he recalled her easy control of the stallion, her poise and her courageous performance.

His lips were curved in an expression of pleasant reverie when Lillian looked up. "*Please,* Flint," she pleaded, squeezing his arm closer.

Flint glanced across the room toward the Spanish tiled wet bar. "We'll have a drink," he said, putting an arm that didn't allow for argument around her waist and propelling her across the shiny floor to the two soft leather bar stools remaining vacant. He helped her into one of them before ordering drinks, which the bartender presently served on small square napkins with a gold *G* embossed in one corner. Then Flint toasted Lillian with a casual lift of his glass, and drank, acknowledging with a nod the man sitting on the other side of her before setting the glass down on the bar surface again.

The man was a few years older than Flint, attractive, youthfully dressed and wearing an artfully done hairpiece. He glanced at Lillian with approving interest before shaking Flint's outstretched hand. "Hey! How are you doing, Flint? I was just talking to a friend of mine yesterday whose specialty is computer entertainment. He says your latest game is going to be a bigger hit than Space Wizard."

"I'm fine, Ted, and better with that kind of news. I'll keep my fingers crossed that your friend is right. But I'm waiting for public reaction before I celebrate." He indicated Lillian with his gaze. "This is Lillian Globe, Ted. She's interested in an acting career."

Ted looked at Lillian with even more interest and smiled the way someone does when a hearty meal is set before him. "I'm Ted Walker, Lillian. I own McMillan Productions."

Lillian's disappointed pout brightened immediately. She returned the man's smile. "Oh, really?" she said, sipping her Harvey Wallbanger. "Then you must be the Ted Walker responsible for Dixie Halton's career?"

"Yes, I did give her a friendly boost. I'm glad to have played a part."

"A part. I've heard you played much more than a 'part,' Mr. Walker. She's a lucky girl to have someone like you to help her. I did some modeling for *Cosmo* once, but that's all. I've been thinking about switching agents. What do you think?"

"Well, that depends." He slid an elbow onto the bar next to hers. "But a girl like you shouldn't have any trouble getting an agent. I'm sure I know someone who would be interested."

Flint stepped down from his stool. "If you'll excuse me, I'll let the two of you get acquainted," he said smoothly.

Lillian turned back to Flint, her face a study in mixed emotions. "Flint, I . . ."

Ted's hand dropped to her knee. "See you later, Flint," he said.

"Do you have to go?" Lillian asked after him. But Flint had already turned his back and seemed not to have heard as he walked away.

As the applause died down, Jennifer continued down the steps, looking over the glittery crowd that formed sociable clusters around the first floor of the hacienda.

In typical southern California tradition, there was a wide range of dress. Will and Patty DuPont, for instance,

17

perhaps the wealthiest couple present, still wore the same rough jeans and boots they had worn all day at the horse show, though Patty's gold earrings were as genuine as the two-karat marquise diamond worn casually on her middle finger. At the other extreme, many wore elegant designer originals. But, in general, none of them seemed to notice or care what any of the guests wore, as they laughed and chatted and refilled their glasses from the spouting mouths of the silver fountain.

Intellectually, Jennifer knew that she was tired. She was always tired after showing a horse all day. But the music, the people, and, most of all, the day's victory had filled her with an expansive glow and energy that wouldn't have let her sleep.

Going to a white-clothed table, she took a glass and reached down to let the silver fountain fill it with bubbly champagne, while several of the crowd broke away to surround her.

"Jennifer! Congratulations, darling." She was swept into a perfumed embrace, her chest pressed hard against Mrs. Roterclimbs' dazzling ruby pendant cut in the shape of a miniature Arabian horse head. "How proud you must be. How do you manage to win and win! And the National Championship, too!"

"Thank you," Jennifer replied with a smile. "But I haven't won the championship yet."

"How modest you are. But if you do, what then?"

"If I do, then next year I'll start training my own filly, Night Wind. I'm very proud of her."

"Wonderful. Good luck."

"Jennifer! Congratulations!" Jeffrey Adams was toasting her with an upheld glass of sparkling champagne. "No one shows a horse quite like you do."

"Thank you. You did well yourself." Jennifer returned cautiously. "But I was only second place to you, as always," he said.

18

Jennifer noticed a flicker of envy in his eyes, and she lowered her gaze to study the contents of her champagne glass.

Jealousy. She'd learned to contend with it long ago as a child, when people had been jealous of her family's wealth and had assumed that, since her family was rich, she must be happy and pampered. But though she never let anyone guess it, she'd always known that her house wasn't as happy as most, money or not.

She was eight years old when a drunk driver slammed head-on into her mother's car, thereby transforming a once happy woman into an ill-tempered skeleton who had to be treated constantly by a staff of nurses and a never-ending stream of doctors. Casa Contenta, the hacienda her parents had named and recently remodeled into a twentieth-century home with nineteenth-century charm, was anything but "contenta." Now it was a hospital of efficient people who seldom spoke to the little girl except to admonish her for muddy boots or to tell her to be quiet because her mother was having a "bad day."

At first Jennifer had tried to read to her mother and do small things to entertain her and make her more comfortable. But to her pain and chagrin, she found her mother had been replaced by a stranger who rejected any efforts to please, no matter how she or her father tried.

But people adjust, Jennifer realized as she looked back. Her father had become more and more involved with Globe Enterprises, staying away from the house on business for days at a time, and she, who had always loved the pony she had been given for her sixth birthday, found the company of animals could be a haven from the adult problems over which she had no control.

She would stay at the barn for hours, grooming Chester, whom she thought of as her best friend. And later, with the help of Manuel, a ranch hand, she had learned to ride bareback and race across the pastures like the wind. And then one day her father told her he would be going on a particularly long trip. "I'm leaving you with the Moores, Jennifer. You'll like them. They have horses, too, Arabians, and they're going to go to the National Championships next week. I'm sending you with them."

As usual when he went away, she vainly protested, "I want to go with you!" But she was unexpectedly happy with Mr. and Mrs. Moore, a warm, loving couple with two daughters of eleven and thirteen, and she found herself secretly wishing they were her own family. And by the time they reached the championships, the pain she felt at her own lack was dimmed by her fascination with the beautiful Arabians.

They competed in every kind of event from jumping to working cows. She heard someone call them "versatile." But she thought of them simply as "marvelous" as she watched them compete under the sparkling glow of the arena lights.

She loved them all—the bays, sleek brown with glistening black manes and tails, chestnuts with stockings of flashing white that pranced on fine legs, blacks, colored dark as ravens' wings and burnished to a fathomless glimmer, and grays, steel covered by silver dapples numerous as the stars of a thousand desert nights. And as she watched, a dream began to form. And that Christmas, when her father called home from Washington, D.C., where he had gone on one of his business trips, and asked her what she wanted for Christmas, she didn't respond with "You to come back very soon," as she always had before, but answered promptly, "An Arabian horse."

And so Chester, who died that winter of old age, was replaced by Serena, an Arabian mare who became her best friend and carried her not only over the eucalyptus-covered hills of the ranch but also into the show ring of small local horse shows. And so it all began—the long hours of practice, practice, and more practice. And the following year, as Jennifer watched the National Championship jumping class, she thought the horses seemed more beautiful than ever. Misty-eyed, she looked on as the blue ribbon and silver tray were awarded and photographers' flashes dazzled the scene with splashes of light. And in her deepest heart she wished with all her might that someday—*she* would be in the winner's circle.

At the time, however, she knew it was an impossible dream. She had learned to jump small barriers in the back pasture, but she didn't have a horse who could possibly win a championship. It was only years later, when she was nearly eighteen and they bred Serena to a National Champion jumper and Desert King was born, that she knew she had a chance. And when she first saw the fiery black colt break free of his mother, jumping to his spindly legs the moment he was born and cantering about his stall when less than ten minutes had passed, she knew *he* was the one.

She never imagined at that time that her parents would both be dead so soon. They had routinely flown off together for her mother to see another specialist, and plane crashes were never expected. She never expected the truth about the ranch, either.

It was not in her father's name, she was told after the funeral, as she sat black-clad in her uncle's office. It was in the name of Globe Enterprises. "For tax reasons," her uncle had explained. And, surprised as she was, Jennifer had appreciated it when her uncle did not evade the truth as her father always had, but told her exactly how high the losses for Globe Enterprises had been.

No wonder her father had been working so hard and had been so preoccupied, she thought, reading the charts and figures she was given. And when her uncle offered to buy her a small beach house or condo to live in, she had refused.

"I won't be a burden," she had said, full of optimism

and energy. "I'm perfectly capable of getting a job and supporting myself. But running this ranch and horse breeding and showing are what I know best. Give me some time and I promise I'll have this ranch making enough money to recover all its losses."

And so the dream had taken on a new dimension, and for the three years since then she had managed the ranch and shown the horses as if her survival depended on it—because she knew it did.

She had bought three new mares first, borrowing money to purchase stud fees to the previous National Champion, Fire Fly, and selling the resulting foals for enough so she began breaking even. Then she concentrated her energy on Desert King, working the stallion carefully, easily. For the last year, he had been unbeatable; his legs remained sound and his disposition eager. Now suddenly the dream was within her grasp. And by winning she would not only fulfill her childhood dream but would earn the right to think of the ranch as one of the Globe family's *successful* enterprises, and know that she was responsible for making it so.

She glanced up from her champagne glass and back at Jeff Adams and smiled good naturedly. Well, if she won the championship then she wouldn't care if everyone in the whole world was jealous.

Her uncle appeared then, offering his arm and taking her from group to group and introducing her to his friends, who all smiled and offered the proper amenities and congratulations, which she accepted with equal politeness. A toast was proposed to her future success. Glasses were raised and the small group was sipping together when a tingling at the back of her neck made Jennifer turn and look around the room.

The main room of the hacienda was large and rectangular with a fireplace of adobe brick at the far end, Indian rugs scattered over the polished wooden floors, and fine leather furniture arranged at comfortable intervals. Her aunt had added to its beauty with several plentiful arrangements of red roses in large ceramic blue vases and the patio at the center of the house was strung with lights.

The band had taken a break and someone was playing ragtime on the piano while Dean Lawrence and Curtis Williams danced wildly with their two blond dates.

Appetizers were arranged on long tables and, looking over the offering of canapes, caviar, and cheese arranged around crackers, guacamole dip and veggies and finger-sized french pastries, Jennifer selected a cream cheese puff and popped it into her mouth, still aware of the strange feeling prickling her senses.

She scanned the room in the opposite direction, past the doors to the smaller family room and the open double front doors, before she found herself looking directly into the gaze of a man leaning against the frame of the open door—a tall man whose tanned face held an aura of vigorous masculinity, a confidence and power as blatant as a slap.

Automatically she swallowed the cheese puff, though she continued to observe him, noting that his hair was wavy, brown, and worn in a casual windblown style that suggested an athletic life. His nose was not small or narrow, but straight, with well-formed nostrils. His jaw was wide and square and saved from harshness by a pair of dimple grooves on either side of his mouth that suggested a boyish air when he smiled as he was doing now.

He wore a plaid western shirt stretched to the limit by the breadth of his shoulders, and slacks that were belted at his narrow waist with tooled leather and a silver conch buckle. The slacks were expensive and, judging by the way they molded his muscular thighs, custom made. And though at that moment Jennifer couldn't place him, she had the impression they had met before.

He did not look away either, and their gazes locked as

he observed her with curious appraisal. The small crowd of admiring women surrounding him laughed at a remark he made, though the focus of his attention never left her. Then, excusing himself, he strode purposefully toward her.

She held her ground, though all her instincts and emotions seemed suddenly on guard as she was forced to lift her chin high to look into his face. "I'd like to introduce myself, Jennifer," he said, his voice warm and resonant. "My name is Flint Michaels." The light in the centers of his eyes penetrated hers for an instant as he extended a large tanned hand. It was impossible not to return his smile or allow her own hand to be engulfed briefly in his sure clasp. "After sitting with your uncle at the horse show this afternoon and watching you ride I feel like we're already friends," he finished.

*Charisma,* Jennifer thought, withdrawing her hand. It was in the confident carriage of his head, his striking handsomeness, and the way he looked at her. Yes, that's why she had thought she knew him—his looks, even the way he carried himself made him seem like Dirk, conceited, irresistible Dirk, who likewise was typically surrounded by women.

Jennifer eyed the stranger. Normally she avoided men who reminded her of Dirk. But tonight, perhaps because of her victory that day, she somehow did not want to simply ignore him and instead began considering a way to let him know that, while other women might fall at his feet like green riders off an unbroken horse, *she* wasn't one of them.

"Friends?" she said, with her eyebrows arched and the hint of a challenge in her voice. "I'm not sure we can be friends."

"No? You have certain criteria?"

"Don't most people?"

"Yes. I guess to one extent or another. What are yours?"

She started to answer but the band suddenly began a primitive rock beat that precluded conversation and Flint Michaels raised his voice over it to ask, "Would you like to dance?"

Now I'm supposed to jump at the chance, Jennifer thought, looking at the large polished dance floor whose dark wood glimmered darkly in the lights turned intimately low. She considered turning him down flat. She really shouldn't, couldn't have anything to do with him. Yet his very presence challenged her in a basic, compelling way that she couldn't ignore. So, accepting his invitation, she casually walked toward the dance floor.

It was a fast dance, and the dancers were so crowded together they could only stand shoulder to shoulder, chest to chest, and keep the beat with a vertical kind of bobbing.

Being five feet, nine inches, Jennifer felt tall with most men, but beside this one she had a new sensation of being actually petite. Or possibly it was his overbearing attitude.

It was a long dance and the music was so loud they couldn't converse. She could only stand a scant six inches from him and move to the rhythm, aware each moment of the faint musk of his shaving soap, the coordinated, easy movements of his large muscular body, and his eyes studying her with friendly interest.

Flint Michaels. Yes, he is a lot like Dirk, she thought, his presence recalling with a dart of pain the part of her past that she always resisted remembering. Dirk. The "God" of her college campus. He too had had that special charisma, that smile which was impossible not to return, that sense of power, immediate and penetrating. She had given herself to him completely, innocently, believing that while her life until then had been full of pain, at last she had found someone who would love her as deeply as she loved him. But Dirk had used her—seduced her, then abandoned her to go on to another "conquest." Jennifer had vowed *never* to make the same mistake again, never to risk all that agony. And, as the years passed, she hadn't. Instead she let all her time and interest be absorbed by the horses, limiting her relations with men to friendship and dismissing with icy aloofness any of Dirk's type who happened to come her way.

Under the cover of the dancing and music Jennifer studied Flint Michaels. Yes, definitely this man was "that" type—a user. No doubt he was as skilled at having his way with women as Dirk had been. And in spite of herself she couldn't help but wonder what it would be like if she did let him chase her, just a little, just enough to deflate that big ego of his. Then, later tonight, she would let him know that he didn't appeal to her at all.

She smiled inwardly as the idea took root. *After all,* she told herself, *I'm a grown woman now and* two *can play this game.*

26

# CHAPTER TWO

The band played on, the guitars, the saxophone, the singer's soulful voice belting out a last chorus. Then, with a roll of drums and a last wail of the sax, it was over.

"Thank you," Jennifer said, looking up at him, a slight smile on her lips, as she turned and slipped away between two couples before he could answer.

She tried not to grin when he followed. All was going according to plan until she ran into her aunt at the edge of the dance floor.

"Jennifer, Flint!" The tall grayhaired woman greeted them, a glow of warmth in her brown eyes, her English accent unfaded despite twenty years of California living. "So I see you have introduced yourselves."

"Yes," Jennifer replied. "We were just . . . dancing."

"Good. It's nice to see both of you having fun. Oh, Jennifer, please be sure to show Flint the stable. Your uncle didn't get a chance this afternoon."

Glancing over at Flint, Jennifer let her long lashes come down in a thick veil to shield her eyes. "Of course I'd be glad to show him the stables, although I doubt if Flint would be interested," she said, giving Flint a subtle yet inviting smile.

"Of course he would," her aunt interjected before Flint could speak. "He's a Texan and grew up on a ranch. Of course he's interested in horses. Oh, I see your uncle waving at me—see you two later."

27

Jennifer smiled as her aunt departed, then glanced at Flint, letting her eyes beckon before she moved away from the others to the champagne fountain so not to be overheard.

Taking a crystal glass from the table, she held it under the bubbling fountain, then lifted it toward him. "Champagne?" she asked.

He nodded, taking the glass from her hand. She knew he was watching her as she turned to fill one for herself. Already the atmosphere between them was intense. When she was younger she had usually been unaware of this tension between herself and a man. But now she knew better. Now she knew when a man found her attractive, and this one was clearly taking the bait.

He touched her glass, the crystal making a bell-like ring. "To your success," he said, his baritone low and deep.

Jennifer laughed lightly at the irony of the toast. "All right," she said, noticing again the confidence in his face as they raised their glasses and their gazes met over the rim. "To my success."

They drank.

There was a pause while he waited for her to speak, and when she didn't he said, "Congratulations on your performance this afternoon. You're the finest rider I've ever seen."

"That's nice of you to say. But the rider is only part of a team. Desert King is a wonderful horse," she replied, letting the conversation pass back to him.

As he took another sip of the champagne his eyes flickered from her lips to the single pearl at her throat and farther down to the curve of her breasts, and finally to her left hand, before he spoke again.

"Your aunt was right," he said. "Your uncle didn't show me the stables."

His examination, however subtle, irritated her and put the light of a challenge in her eyes as she asked, "Would you really like me to show you?" delighted by the double meaning and smiling again, her eyes never leaving his.

"I'm very interested," he said, with an answering light.

"Really. When do you want to go?"

"Now. I was impressed with what I saw today. I'd like to know more." And now it was up to her to consider if his words held a second interpretation.

"Fine," she said, after pausing only a moment, feeling more determined than ever to lower him a peg. "The barn is at the back of the house."

She walked ahead of him, swinging her long blond ponytail and giving her slender hips an extra swirl. Oh, she would have him eating out of her hand before ten minutes had passed, she told herself as they moved out the patio doors and through the garden, then passed beyond a wrought-iron gate that Flint closed behind them with a small squeak of its hinges.

The barn door was visible in the distance, a single light dimly illuminating the wide double doors.

Jennifer led the way on the gravel path that wound toward it. She made no further attempt at conversation and the only sounds were made by his boots crunching against the path and the lighter tread of her high heels, which she now realized were completely inadequate on the rocky surface. And as the silence stretched out, she found herself more acutely aware of him, his long strides that he slowed to accommodate her slower pace, his towering height, those eyes that she felt sweep her frame, and something she could only describe as an aura of confidence and power that she found more annoying every minute. So, wanting to somehow change the focus, she said, "Why are you interested in Arabians?"

"I wasn't, until this afternoon," he said. "But your uncle and I have had business dealings for years. He told me his niece would be showing at a horse show in Santa

Barbara and invited me to attend. It was a good excuse for some time off."

"You're on vacation, then?" Jennifer asked, with the disconcerting thought that her uncle might have also asked him to stay the weekend. She suddenly realized she knew nothing at all of Uncle Walter's plans. As usual, she hadn't asked. She was always just happy to see them when they stopped in on occasion, staying the night and often giving parties.

"I haven't decided," he answered. "Fortunately, my office staff functions perfectly without my constant presence. I simply keep in touch by phone."

"Oh. I see," she said, hearing the uncertainty in her own voice before covering it with a smile. "How nice for you. Then you must travel a lot."

"Not as much as I used to. It's a beautiful world, but southern California is my favorite place. You've lived here all your life?"

"Yes. My parents were born here, and my grandparents too." Even in the dark she was aware of the power in those green animal eyes that gazed at her with interest. And now I'm supposed to be flattered to death that he's paying attention to me, she thought.

Ahead of them the path narrowed, so she was forced to walk closer to him. A few moments of silence had passed when their hands unexpectedly touched—once, and then again.

She recoiled as the warm contact of his fingers sent waves of rippling disturbances racing through her like the vibrations of a tuning fork against her flesh. And when he remained close behind her, so close Jennifer could feel the heat of him, she moved off the path onto the lawn bordering it.

At once she felt more comfortable, particularly since on the higher level he didn't seem so tall. Wrapped up in her thoughts, she was not paying close attention to where she stepped, so she didn't see the large rock in her way until it caught her toe.

She would have gone to her knees except for the strong arm that instantly circled her waist, supporting her until she regained her footing. "Thank you," she said, aware again of his disturbing size, of her own helplessness within the strength of his grasp, and of the unyielding hardness of the body against which she was pressed. And when her feet were firmly on the ground again and he still hadn't released her, she said firmly, "I'm fine now, thank you."

A moment passed while the muscular arm didn't budge and she remained there, her breasts pressed hard into his wide chest. Then he let her go.

Impulsively, Jennifer wanted to release the harsh words that clamored within her. Yet feeling she would only seem ridiculous and ungrateful for his help, she controlled herself and moved further off the path, concentrating on the footing and trying to satisfy herself by considering just how his face would look when she finally let him know just how unattractive she really thought he was.

It was only a short distance to the stable, and when at last they entered the dim light of the barn a familiar voice came from the shadows of the stall.

"*Buenas noches,* Señorita Jennifer."

"Ah, Manuel. I'm so glad you're here," she said sincerely as a tall, angular Mexican with dark sparkling eyes and a head of straight white hair stepped from the interior of the stall into the light.

"I wondered whether you'd come and see Night Wind tonight."

"Manuel, this is Flint Michaels," Jennifer said. "He's a friend of my uncle's."

"*Con mucho gusto,*" Manuel said, his dark eyes scanning the taller man.

"And I'd like you to meet Manuel, Flint," she con-

31

tinued, turning her head from one man to the other. "Manuel has worked for the ranch as long as I can remember, and he's a better man with horses than anyone I've ever met."

"I see. Then I'm honored to meet you," Flint said, extending his wide hand to clasp Manuel's smaller gnarled one.

"Uncle Walter wanted me to show Flint the stables," Jennifer explained.

"Then you go ahead, Señorita. The horses are down for the night. That Desert King, he's still rarin' to go but Night Wind she's just sad and lookin' for you over her stall door all day long."

"Poor girl," Jennifer said, not able to hide the slight smile of pleasure at the news that her favorite horse had missed her. "I'll work her first thing in the morning."

"You do that, Señorita," Manuel said. "*Hasta luego*. But now I will put these old bones to a mattress." His toughened palm raised in a wave as he started up the golden sawdust aisle toward the small house beyond the barn that had been his for thirty years.

"*Hasta luego*, Manuel," Jennifer replied, leading Flint to where the horses stood with heads stretched out into the aisle over the low half doors that confined them in box stalls.

At the first stall door, she paused, sliding back a metal bolt to open it and reveal a dappled gray mare heavy with foal whose wide brown eyes watched them alertly. "This is Serena, our oldest and possibly finest broodmare," Jennifer explained in a matter-of-fact tone. "We're looking forward to the foal next month by a pure Egyptian stallion," she continued as she walked into the stall. Forgetting for a moment about her annoyance with Flint, she stroked the mare's long graceful neck with love in her every movement. She kept her back turned as she con-

32

tinued caressing the mare, and when he made no comment, she said over her shoulder, "Do you like her?"

"Very much," came Flint's voice. And something in it made her turn to find that his eyes were not on the mare, but on her.

For a long moment their gazes met, an energy passing between them that challenged her in an intimate way. He certainly did not waste time getting to the point, Jennifer thought. A prickle of warning ran up her spine and when he moved again, she thought for a horrible two seconds that he was going to take her in his arms. But then, to her relief, he walked to the opposite side of Serena and ran a gentle hand along the top of the mare's back, slowly down each leg, and finally along her neck in the careful assessing way of a man who knows horses.

"She's a beauty," he said at last, giving the mare's ears a scratch. As if she understood, Serena nuzzled him, her velvety nose running over his hand and up his arm with friendly affection.

"She likes you," Jennifer observed, feeling a needling sense of betrayal.

"Most females think I'm passable when they get to know me," he said, fondling the mare. "Although some take longer than others."

Jennifer's gaze shot to his face, ricocheted off his probing emerald gaze and moved back to the mare.

"Really?" And a hint of disgust entered her tone, though she tried to keep her voice pleasant. "Maybe they find you too forward."

Flint continued stroking the mare's neck. "Maybe. But they usually respond well once they find out I'm someone who understands them."

"And I suppose they then follow you around and eat out of your hand?" Jennifer commented, balling her fists and sliding them behind her back.

"Something like that," he agreed, a hint of a smile forming around his mouth, his eyes twinkling into hers.

His self-assurance was galling, and it severely tested Jennifer's self-control. But, determined not to be forced into a scene, she ignored the remark and walked silently out of the stall and on to the next, jerking back the bolt with a snap and opening the door.

Inside, a shiny black horse looked up from his generous manger of alfalfa. "This is Desert King," Jennifer said, her voice tight with tension. "He's the one I jumped this afternoon. He's the best jumping Arabian we've ever bred. He's smaller than thoroughbred jumpers, of course, but he makes up for his size with courage. In a month we'll compete for the National Championship."

She didn't pause longer for him to comment but shut the door with a bang and moved to the next stall, where a high-pitched whinny greeted her and a young horse stepped closer to nudge her arm with its nose. In spite of her annoyance with Flint, Jennifer smiled and ran her hands over the filly's soft nose and up to her ears.

"And this is my filly, Night Wind," she said with pride. In another few years I'm hoping she'll be a National Champion.'

"I see," was all he said. And Jennifer's aggravation returned full force when Night Wind walked over and nuzzled in his pockets with friendly curiosity.

Absently Flint stroked the filly's back as a frown formed between his brows. Then, as if he'd made some kind of decision, he patted the filly one final time before saying, "She's certainly a winner. I'm sure you'll have no trouble making her a champion."

"Thank you," Jennifer said, giving the filly a last affectionate pat, from the crest of her shiny neck down the soft hair to her shoulder, before stepping outside the stall.

He followed as she showed him the rest of the horses. She was relieved that he made no further advances toward

34

her but instead turned his attention to the horses, approaching them with interest, complimenting all of them on their strong points and yet able to see subtle imperfections. He even surprised her by his knowledge of Arabian horse jargon, referring to one horse's "dry head" when he complimented the delicate sculpture of her fine bonestructure. Then he was silent again as they walked back toward the hacienda.

The moon had risen, so a tiny crescent rode low in the purple autumn sky, its fine shape blurred by a light fog that carried the fragrance of freshly mown hay. "You really do know something about horses," she said, wanting to banish the silence that had become somehow intimate.

Even in the dim light, she could see the flash of white teeth and the sparkle of his eyes. "I'll consider that a real compliment, coming from you."

Her chin jerked up. "Oh? Do I seem short of compliments, Mr. Michaels?" she asked, trying to keep her voice pleasant.

"You seem a lot of things."

"Really? Such as?"

"Such as vulnerable, yet very strong. Polite, but not so polite you aren't also rude. Flirtatious yet, at the moment, testy as a badger trapped in his hole," he finished, with the hint of a drawl.

"I'm not 'testy,' " she said, embarrassed that he could read her so easily.

His head cocked at an angle. "That adds to the list. I imagine you normally tell the truth. But you aren't now, at least not all of it."

"Are you calling me a liar?" she asked, staring directly into his face.

Again his white teeth came into view. "What I'm asking for is more of the truth."

"Really," Jennifer said, sarcasm entering her tone as

she felt herself being cornered. "I'm sorry. But maybe you're just used to other women treating you differently."

His lips compressed slightly and his head angled again in acquiescence. "I'd admit to that," he agreed. "But I'm most interested in understanding you."

"Are you?" she said, then turned abruptly and starting toward the house again.

She hadn't taken two steps when he stopped her, a large hand encircling her bare upper arm and holding her back in a grip that didn't hurt but wouldn't yield. Rather than struggle, she stopped and faced him.

"All right," she said, after they had stared at each other too long. "What is it you want to understand?"

"For starters, why you are smiles one minute and darts the next. But I'd like to know much more. You must realize I find you very attractive," he finished simply.

Jennifer smiled nervously. Someone had once told her the best defense was a good offense, so now she said, "Attractive? And now I guess I should be flattered, right?"

"No."

"Then what?"

"You could answer me."

His expression was determined and unyielding. Wanting only to stop the conversation, she said, "It's none of your business how I feel." She jerked away. "Can't you just forget it? Why are you so persistent?"

In the pale moonlight, amusement crinkled the corners of his eyes so it seemed he was just playing with her. "I guess persistence is one of my faults, although I'm sure *you* could probably name a lot more. But I make a point of never giving up on anything until I'm given a sufficient reason."

Getting a crick in her neck from looking so far up and wondering just how much those green eyes could read, Jennifer turned away. He was infuriating. And refusing to say more, she hurried faster along the path, the gravel grabbing at her high heels as they sank deep into the thickness of small stones.

"Oh damn! I don't believe it!" she said then as she suddenly found herself on the ground, her ankle burning painfully.

Immediately he was kneeling at her side, his wide forehead frowning with concern as, with matter-of-fact familiarity, he took her ankle in his hand, undid the straps, and slipped off the shoe.

Jennifer started to protest, but when she tried to stand, the pain in her ankle turned her first word into a grimace and she sat down again with a hissing intake of breath.

"It's not broken," he said, examining it with competent fingers that ran completely around her ankle and partway up her calf. Again she started to pull away, but his firm grip made it impossible to move. "It looks like a sprain," he continued. "If you get ice on it right away I don't think it will be serious."

"Damn!" Jennifer said again. "I have such weak ankles. I should have known . . ." She didn't go on aloud but rather to herself, cursing silently the impulse that had brought her out here in the beginning.

The pressing of his fingers made her grimace again. "Yes. It's pulled," he confirmed. "Come on. Put your arms around me. I'll carry you to the house."

Before she could protest, she was up in his arms, carried effortlessly against the hard curving of his chest.

"I want to get down!"

He didn't answer.

"I'm serious!" she insisted. And when that didn't work she said more coldly: "Mr. Michaels. I can walk."

"There's no reason for you to. I'm perfectly capable of carrying you," was all he said as they continued moving through the darkness with his swinging gait.

"I'm aware of that," she said in a hard forceful voice. "But I *want* to walk."

He did set her down then, and she winced as her toe touched the ground.

"Why are you being so stubborn?" he asked, seeing her mouth twist with pain. "You need to be carried and I can carry you. You'll only injure yourself more by walking. And if you hurt it more now, what about the championship? You need your ankles to ride."

The logic was plain in his words. And what was she going to do—tell him she would rather injure herself again than feel so utterly overwhelmed by his muscular chest, the warm, good, smell of his masculine body, the strength of his arms surrounding her in an unbreakable grip? Anyway, the initial numbing shock of her ankle had worn off now and it was hurting worse than before.

"All right," she said, although the tone of her voice didn't give an inch. "Have it your own way."

She didn't need to say more. Already he was swinging her up again and striding long and sure toward the house. But when they reached the patio she said, "This is far enough. I can make it on my own from here."

They were nearly to the double doors that opened out onto the vast lawns surrounding the hacienda, and, glancing inside the house, Jennifer noticed the lights had been dimmed. Some guests had departed and the party had reached a more intimate stage, with the guests lounging on the comfortable furniture, propping themselves with the fiber-woven pillows and chatting in lower voices. The band had stopped playing, and in one corner a couple was kissing, in romantic oblivion to the rest of the party.

It was a scene that in her present state of mind held no attraction and, deciding the time had come to relieve herself of Flint Michaels, she said, "I'm not going in. I'll just go to my room from here."

He just looked at her. The unrelenting hold of his arms

38

made her continue. "I'm really very tired and I need to get up early to exercise my filly. So, if you'll excuse me?" she finished, with one slender eyebrow slightly raised. He didn't look disappointed in the least, and neither did he put her down. "I'd like you to stay," he said simply. "Anyway"—he indicated the party with a movement of his chin—"your aunt and uncle will miss you."

"No. I'm certain they won't. They're busy with their friends, and I'll have time with them in the morning. But if they should ask, you can tell them I've gone to bed. I'm sure they'll understand. And anyway I'd like to put ice on this in privacy."

It was true, she was tired and would prefer to ice her ankle away from public scrutiny, but she was beginning to feel a growing vulnerability in his arms, like a fox that had baited the hound but now found itself losing ground.

She should have known it would only bring trouble to flirt with him. She sighed. It was true that she had made a life work of taking on hazardous challenges. She had never balked at riding the wildest of horses, for instance. But she should have learned that men, particularly men like this, were one kind of hazard to leave alone.

When still he gave no sign of letting her down she said, "I'd like you to put me down." He assessed her a moment. Then at last he nodded, with a smile. "I guess I understand. How would it look for the day's heroine to show up back at the party with proof she's not made of steel?" he teased. "Although it's a fact that I think you should start considering."

"I suppose you're right," she said, trying to be agreeable now that she was going to escape. "My bedroom is just up those stairs." She indicated a stairway at the side of the patio that led to the upper floor and a vine-covered landing that overlooked them. "Just put me down and I'll make it."

He didn't seem even to consider her request before he turned and climbed up the stairs, taking them two at a time in spite of her weight.

"Put me down now," she said. But he acted as if she hadn't said a word as they continued up, up, up where it was darker and the cricket's cries surrounded them.

She thought of screaming but didn't, realizing how stupid and hysterical she would seem. Oh, he was impossible! Then they were above the crowd, suddenly isolated in the shadows of the landing outside her room and, turning the handle, he opened the door and entered, flipping on the light.

Her bedroom with its heavy Spanish furniture was illuminated by two swag lamps flanking her wide, queen-size bed. A wave of embarrassment swept her as she saw the open dresser drawers with dangling stockings and the haphazard closet. Housework had never been her strong suit. But this discomfiture was dimmed by the growing sense of danger, and her arms, which she had held loosely around his neck, now pushed him away.

He let her legs down easily so she stood on one foot, but the upper half of her body was still held close by an arm across her back, and he was studying her with those smoky emerald eyes, really too large and beautiful for a man, and much too knowing now as he said, "You still haven't answered my question."

"I don't have to answer any of your questions, Mr. Michaels," she said. "I appreciate your help but now I want you to go."

"I will go," he said. "After you answer my question."

"What question?" she asked harshly.

"I'm curious to know why you were full of smiles and swaying hips before I called your bluff, and yet madder than hell at me now."

"That's ridiculous! And I'm not obligated to answer any

of your questions," she said, although the truth of his accusation sent a flush across her face.

Of course she knew he wouldn't let it go at that. But she was still shocked when he said, "I mean, plainly put, that you are a *tease,* Jennifer Globe."

The word hit her like a slap. No one had ever called her such a thing, let alone a man like this, who was no doubt a master of insincerity himself. And it was worse to realize that now his reaction was justified.

"Oh?" she said, with narrowing eyes. "And how would you characterize yourself, Mr. Michaels?"

"Teased—thoroughly. But I don't need to tell you that, do I? I can see you're experienced enough at playing this game to be able to tell yourself."

"Not as 'experienced' as *you* obviously are, Mr. Michaels," she sneered, with all the anger she felt. "But if I haven't fallen into your arms it's because I don't find you attractive."

"No?"

He was amused; the slight curve to his well-etched mouth told her so. But the very closeness of that mouth, the look in his eyes, made her suddenly grab for something more tangible. "And anyway," she added with the tone of a final thrust, "I have a boyfriend—someone I'm serious about. So you see I have no interest in anyone else."

The satisfaction she planned to gain from this moment of rejection didn't come, though the twitch of a muscle in his jaw told her she had hit the right nerve. "I see," he commented. "Tell me about him."

Jennifer wanted to tell him it was none of his business. But, seeing this as an opening to make her lack of interest completely clear, she said, "His name is Richard Hobbes. He's a researcher for a museum in San Francisco."

"Really?" he said evenly. "And you're serious about him?"

"Yes. We're . . . engaged." she said, crossing her fingers against the lie but feeling forced into it.

"He lives here?"

"No. But we see each other every few weeks. This week, for instance, he's organizing a display of Indian artifacts in Santa Barbara, and we'll be seeing each other."

*There,* she thought. *That should discourage him, even though Richard and I are really hardly more than friends.*

"Every few weeks? You don't mind being separated from him that much?"

Again he was moving her into a corner, and bristling, she said, "Richard has his work and I have the horses. We have a mature relationship that doesn't need the constant presence of the other."

"Hmmm." It was a low, calculating note. "That all seems clear and logical. And you love him?"

"Yes," she said, losing patience. "But I imagine you think I should be thrilled that *you* find me 'attractive.' "

"Not especially." He was frowning now. "I find any number of women physically attractive. But initially I thought there might be something more between us." He shrugged. "Sometimes I make mistakes."

"I'm sorry that's what you thought. But there is nothing 'more' between us."

There was a pause as he seemed to assess her words. "Yes. I see," was all he said before his arms suddenly tightened to pull her hard against his shoulder and his other hand crossed his body to capture her chin. "In that case, one kiss won't hurt," he continued—"that is, if you really do *love* this Richard of yours."

Then his mouth was on hers, hard at first, parting her lips, his tongue running across the outside of her clenched teeth, then softer, along the interior of her lips, teasing, coaxing.

It was an unexpected sensation, a whirlpool that rose to

42

titillate, to compel. Vaguely, she thought, *he can't, I won't let him*. But she couldn't move. Just as before, she was helpless in the firm strength of his arms. And suddenly her teeth were no longer a barrier as, more demanding now, he took her mouth in deep passionate possession.

A persistent voice at the back of her mind wanted her to remain stiff and unyielding, but her head swirled and her body seemed unwilling to resist, and it curved against his.

Slowly, then, his arms relaxed and he held her away from him.

Her legs were unsteady, and to her embarrassment she swayed into him. He didn't speak but continued to watch her, and when she found her voice again she said, "You had no right to do that. I didn't want you to."

A sparkle was coming to twinkle his eyes. "No? But I was curious," he said.

"Curious?"

"Yes. I wanted to know if you're really as unreachable as you like to act. It's good to know I wasn't so mistaken after all." He smiled. "Good night, until tomorrow," he finished, then turned and started toward the door.

Something in his retreating back made her recover herself. "I won't be seeing you tomorrow or any day," she said.

At the doorway he turned. "Yes. I'm afraid you will. Your uncle has invited me to stay here as his house guest until tomorrow and then . . . well, who knows after that. Good night," he said again. "And I'll have someone bring you ice."

Jennifer stood staring at the door long after he had closed it. Then she sat heavily on the bed. *He had no right to kiss me like that,* she told herself. Why hadn't she stopped him, screamed, at least slapped the confident look right off his face?

A knock on the door interrupted her internal tirade.

"Yes," she answered, fearing the worst. She was relieved to hear her aunt's voice saying, "It's just me, Jennifer. I brought you some ice."

"Oh come in, Aunt Victoria," she said, trying to brighten her voice.

Victoria Globe came in immediately, a bowl of ice held gingerly in her arms to prevent spotting her high-style, nubby plum pants suit. Over her shoulder was a thick terry-cloth towel and a plastic sack. She set the bowl on the night stand.

"Flint told me you hurt your ankle. I hope it's nothing serious," she said with concern.

"No, not serious," Jennifer said, removing her panty hose and unzipping her dress to pull over her head. "If I use ice tonight I should be able to walk on it tomorrow. I've had this happen before."

Her aunt assisted by handing her a robe as she peered at the ankle. "It doesn't look too swollen now," she offered.

"No, it's going to be fine. Really."

"Oh, I'm sure it is. But Flint wanted me to bring the ice immediately. He seemed quite concerned."

"Was he?" Jennifer said, imagining how solicitous Flint must have been.

"Yes," her aunt replied. "Tell me. How was your tour of the stables?"

Jennifer sat down, the pain of her ankle, the tension of the evening making her suddenly aware of a permeating weariness. She wanted to confide in the older woman, but how could she explain her feelings without bringing up the topic of Flint? Her evening had already been upsetting enough. So veering away altogether from the topic of Flint, she said, "The horses looked fine. Manuel takes wonderful care of them, so I never have to worry. He's a real gem."

44

"Yes, of course," her aunt agreed. "But I was asking more to find out what you think of Flint."

Jennifer took the plastic ice pack from her aunt and began filling it with ice cubes. "I don't think we really have much in common."

"Hmmm . . . I'm surprised. Flint is really very fond of horses. I expected the two of you to hit it off."

Jennifer filled the sack with ice cubes and wrapped it in a towel. Then, positioning herself in a chair beside her bed, she fitted the ice around her ankle. "No. I guess all people who like horses don't necessarily like each other."

"Yes, I suppose you're right. But I was hoping. Your uncle likes him and, well, I thought you might consider him good husband material."

The look of surprise and horror that came to her niece's face was enough to make Victoria automatically withdraw a step.

"Husband! I'm not sure I *ever* intend to get married. But if I do it would *never* be to a man like that!"

"Really?" Victoria Globe said. Then she sighed, seeming suddenly very young and wistful as she said, "Oh, maybe I'm old fashioned in my tastes. But I find a big man like that extremely attractive. I like that bold look in a man's eye. And then he has all that money." She sighed again. "But I guess not everyone likes the same things. I just thought you might find him interesting and I think Flint has reached an age when he might be inclined to settle down. Lillian, of course, is crazy about him, as anyone can see. But I think someone else would suit him better, someone more serious . . . Oh, well." She waved her hand. "I've got to get back to my guests. You feel better, dear." Her aunt's hand caressed her cheek. "And do think about what I said. You might give him a second consideration." She picked up the bowl and headed toward the door. When she reached it she turned. "Sometimes first impressions are deceiving. I have a feeling you're going to see a lot more of him."

She closed the door behind her, but the last look on her face made Jennifer think there was some hidden meaning behind her words.

As it turned out, there was—but she didn't receive *that* shock until the following morning.

# CHAPTER THREE

"Sold! No . . . no, that's impossible!" Jennifer said, staring at her uncle across the wide oak desk. She gripped the arms of her chair, her fingernails making crescent marks in the thick leather upholstering, and tried to compose herself. "You're teasing me . . . joking." But she knew he wasn't, not about this. A feeling rose up from her stomach as she tried to control the growing fullness in her throat. She didn't interrupt her uncle again as he went on.

"I'm sorry, Jennifer. I know how much you love the ranch. Believe me, it was only a last resort to sell. But I don't need to tell you the Globe fortune isn't even a fraction of what it once was. Inflation and energy costs have driven several of our key companies out of business. As head of the family, I have to think of all of our futures. The ranch hasn't made a profit for years now, and a buyer has made me an offer that is impossible to turn down. I hope you can understand."

Jennifer crossed her long legs and forced back hot tears. Yes, she understood perfectly. For ten years now Walter had managed the family financial affairs so poorly that even her aunt had once said, "Your uncle means well but he wasn't meant to be a businessman. He's just not suited for this kind of thing."

But nevertheless, since he had inherited the position of head of the family, he had insisted on handling everything himself, and now things had gone from bad to worse and something had to be sold.

She took a breath, trying to ease the tightness in her chest.

"I know the ranch hasn't been making money," she began, trying to control the cutting emotions in her chest, "But if only you'd waited until after the championship. If Desert King wins there'll be plenty of people willing to pay a stud fee of ten thousand a mare for breeding rights. With that kind of money we could've run this ranch with a handsome profit. I've been planning this for years. Why didn't you discuss this with me?"

Her uncle leaned forward and patted her hand, a useless, patronizing gesture that made her want to scream.

"I'm sorry, honey. Maybe I should have, but I didn't want to worry you. Anyway, Desert King might not win the championship, and we can't afford to gamble when such a generous offer has been presented."

Jennifer pulled her hand away, clenching the chair arm, her knuckles pale.

"I'm sorry," he said again.

She sighed deeply, blinking back the tears and lifting her chin.

"Tell me what deal you've made."

Walter Globe sat back in his chair and smiled as he said, "Sixty thousand in cash immediately as a down payment for the horses." He did not seem to hear Jennifer gasp as he continued. "Nine-hundred-and-fifty thousand in thirty days for the ranch house and property and the rest at the close of escrow. I've also agreed to turn over possession of the guest house. He wants to move in immediately. It's a stipulation of the deal." He looked more intently at Jennifer. "The important thing to remember, of course, is that this will keep our own position solvent while some of our investments have a chance to recover. I simply couldn't turn this kind of offer down."

Jennifer sat silently in the darkness of the leather chair, her head down, afraid to speak now when she would be rash and emotional and probably say all the angry, bitter things that swirled around her head, things she would regret saying later. She didn't look up until he said again, "I hope you understand."

"I understand that you're doing what you think is best." Her voice was low. "I'm just very sorry it was the ranch that had to go."

A knock on the door interrupted them.

"Come in."

The neat gray head of Sarah, her uncle's longtime secretary, poked in the door. "Excuse me, Mr. Globe," she began, "but Mr. Michaels is here to see you. He wants to go over the details of his contract to buy the ranch."

"Good. Show him in."

For a moment Jennifer felt as if the breath had been knocked out of her. Her stomach knotted, twisting into a tight ball, and a small involuntary gasp passed her lips as the tall man strode in with the confident ease of a conquerer and shook hands with her uncle. Then both men turned to her. "And you two have met, as I recall," her uncle was saying.

"Yes . . . we have," was all Jennifer could say as she fought an urge to slap the handsome face that watched her carefully behind its pleasant smile. This was ridiculous— and really cruel. What a fool she had been! All the time *she* had been showing him the ranch, *he* had been examining it with an eye to buy. Damn him! At least he might have given her some idea of his intention. But no! He had actually let her believe that he really was attracted to her—even said as much. And that kiss, which had given her not entirely unpleasant feelings whenever she had thought of it during that long sleepless night, now made her suddenly feel soiled and ashamed.

She gritted her teeth. She should have known better, of

course. Men like Flint Michaels never did anything but use people to their own ends.

She got up from the chair, drawing herself to full height. "We have met," she began again coldly. "But actually I was just leaving."

"I'd like you to stay, Jennifer," Flint was saying, without moving out of her path to the door. "We need to go over some of the details together since we are going to be neighbors, for the time being anyway."

"Details?" An icy cold challenge was in her eyes. "I'm sure you will handle all the 'details' as you see fit. I think you've done well enough without my help so far."

"Yes, well maybe you two can talk later," Walter interceded, seeking to avoid a confrontation.

"And actually we won't be neighbors for long," Jennifer continued. "The ranch is yours now. Congratulations."

She stepped around him and stalked to the door, opened it and then, as an afterthought, turned and said, "By the way, Mr. Michaels, I think you're very *clever.*

It felt good to slam the door behind her, ignore the pain in her ankle to stalk purposefully down the hall, and keep walking when she heard the door open again and Flint's boot heels hitting the flagstone floor as he came after her.

"Jennifer. I want to talk to you." His voice was firm. But Jennifer didn't even look back as she answered,

"There is nothing to say."

"Yes, there is."

He was still behind her as she started up the stairs.

"Do I have to physically stop you?"

She did stop then and faced him on the landing, hands on hips. "No you don't *have* to stop me! I could stop myself if I wanted to, but I don't. Let's get one thing clear, Mr. Michaels. You may have taken advantage of my uncle and bought this ranch, but *I* don't come along with it! So don't make the mistake of ordering *me* to do *anything!*"

The outburst of anger released all her pent-up emotions.

And suddenly feeling unable to hold back the sobs that threatened to choke her, she turned and half limped, half ran up the stairs, slamming her bedroom door behind her and leaning hard against it.

Her legs were trembling. Taking two slow, lifeless steps to the bed, she threw herself on it full length and muffled her strangled cries in a pillow. The ranch, her ranch, was gone, she thought, aware now of her deep love for the green rolling pastures and miles of white fences, the mares heavy in foal and standing in wild flowers. And her dream of winning the championship—the most important dream of her life. Now it was all gone, never to be hers again, sold to a stranger.

She cried until her pillow was sodden, until her stomach contracted painfully and tears gave way to whimpers. She lay perfectly still for several minutes, wondering vaguely why crying didn't ever help when you most wanted it to. She could cry until she drowned in her own tears and nothing would change. The ranch would still be sold, her hopes for her future destroyed.

The phone ringing beside her bed roused her. Grabbing the receiver, she fumbled to get it to her ear. "Hello."

"Jennifer, is that you?"

"Yes—Richard. When did you get in? Where are you?"

"I'm waiting for you at the shopping mall. You were supposed to meet me at eleven. Don't you remember?"

"I didn't . . . I mean. . . ."

"Hey, are you all right? You sound upset."

"Oh—Richard. The ranch has been sold."

"Sold? Who sold it?"

"Uncle Walter. The family is in financial trouble. They needed the money. This awful man who was at the party last night offered him too much to turn down."

"No! Jennifer! That's terrible. What are you going to do?"

"What can I do? I'm moving out as soon as possible."

51

There was only a brief pause. "You're welcome to move into my place. I'm going to be gone for a month and you're welcome to use it. Anyway, San Francisco might do you good."

Jennifer's temples pounded. "Oh . . . I don't know. Everything just happened and I feel terrible right now. I'm not thinking clearly."

"Well, look." His voice was soothing. "Get ready and come down here to the shopping center. We'll have lunch and talk things over."

Jennifer rubbed her swollen eyes. "I suppose there's no sense in staying around here. Yes . . . all right . . . give me an hour. Browse or something until then."

"Okay. See you later."

Jennifer set down the receiver. Feeling heartsick to the core, she got up and headed for the shower. It took more than an hour to make herself presentable. She listlessly looked through her closet three times, finally pulling out a blue cotton dress with see-through crochet work on the sleeves and neckline. Her makeup was the most painstaking operation of all. But even with great care, her eyes still looked red-rimmed and swollen as she walked along the mall to the middle point.

Richard was waiting there. Putting a steady arm around her, he gave her a kiss on the cheek. He was tall and slim, his tanned features contrasting with his pale blond hair. They had known each other since college, when, finding that they weren't romantically inclined, they had become excellent friends, and now Jennifer was glad for the strong comforting arm that circled her shoulders. It was good to be with someone who knew her well, someone she didn't have to impress or explain things to. Someone who cared.

"Your ankle," he said, noticing her limp.

"Yes, I've hurt it again, but not badly. It'll be fine."

"Okay. Let's sit down here on the bench."

They did, and Jennifer was glad when he didn't urge her

to talk but let her begin in her own time. She began pouring it all out; he was a good listener, not trying to offer useless advice but letting her know he understood as the next few hours passed and the truth slowly sank in.

Oddly, she didn't cry anymore but felt somehow calm, as if for the moment all her emotions had been spent. The ranch was sold. It was taken out of her hands. There was nothing she could do but steel herself to bear it.

"I need to move out from the ranch as soon as I can," she said, trying to think practically. "A clean break will be better. But I don't know where I can keep Night Wind. She's my responsibility and I certainly don't want to leave her on the ranch."

"I have a friend nearby who has a stable," Richard offered. "You can keep her there for the time being." He squeezed her waist. "Listen, Jennifer. You've got some decisions to make, but look at this as an opportunity to make your life better. I think that after this is all worked out things will be fine again. It's true that time heals."

She nodded again, not really believing it, but trying to seem grateful for his support. "Thank you, Richard," she said at last, giving him a hug and kissing his smoothly shaven cheek. "I'm going to be fine. I am. It's just the shock."

He smiled. "Okay. Well, what do you say I drive you to the park and we can spend the rest of the afternoon relaxing?"

"That sounds good," she said. "I always did enjoy feeding those stupid pigeons."

They spent the rest of the afternoon on the grassy strip bordering the water, feeding the numerous birds while they talked of the past and friends and the ranch and Jennifer tried to maintain a reasonably cheerful facade.

Evening found them at a restaurant on a cliff overlooking the rolling white-crested waves of the Pacific. Jennifer ordered Mahi Mahi automatically and Richard, as usual, had Sand Dabs. They didn't talk anymore about the ranch, and Richard launched into a report on the museum's latest dig that had uncovered the remains of an ancient Indian village. And she listened, refusing to think about the ranch, admiring his intelligence and asking questions about his research, making suggestions and trying to be as helpful to him as he always was to her.

"I'm hoping the carbon testing on bone scraps will be twenty thousand years older than any found before," he said as after-dinner drinks were served. "It will prove many of the long-believed theories completely wrong."

"Hmmm," Jennifer acknowledged, her attention having wandered to the profile of a man's head across the restaurant. The room was romantically lit in a soft rosy glow that blurred details so she couldn't see him as well as she could the woman he was with, a honey blonde with a sexy, rumpled Farah Fawcett–type hairdo, and a blouse cut low to reveal her dark tan. Her smile was full of shiny white teeth when she flashed it, which was often, though it seemed she wasn't getting the response she wanted. Reaching across the table, she touched his hand appealingly and smiled again, leaning forward slightly so more pretty cleavage was visible.

The blonde's smile disappeared suddenly. She tilted her head to one side in apparent resignation, then nodded. Gathering her purse, she stood up. He followed suit and remained standing as she kissed her palm and laid it against his cheek. Then she moved away through the restaurant, sliding her slinky body between the tables with a swirl of gently rounded hips.

Richard stared at the girl but Jennifer didn't notice, since her own concentration had never left the tall man who settled the check with his back to her. Though she hadn't yet seen his face, she knew it could only be him. And when their eyes did meet, an electrical current passed between them that seemed to crackle the air.

"Flint!"

Richard leaned closer. "What?"

"Flint," she whispered, feeling absurd since he was still watching her and undoubtedly knew she was talking about him. "Flint Michaels."

"Oh." Richard glanced up. "Yes. I recognize him now. Wasn't he just in *Financial Magazine* as the king of the electronic games business? And look. He's coming to our table." He glanced back at her. "Do you know him?"

"Yes. Last night at the party. He's the one who . . ."

"Good evening. I'm surprised to see you again so soon," Flint said, interrupting her explanation.

Jennifer looked up, only a thin layer of politeness veiling the fury in her eyes, her skin blushing red to the roots of her blond hair. She remembered the lie she had told about being engaged to Richard. How had he shown up like this—as if he had known where she would be? A karate chop to the throat and one to the solar plexus, she thought, recalling from her self-defense class last summer that those were fatal blows. But ultimately she could only go along with the farce of politeness and introduce the two men, watching them exchange formalities and shake hands.

From Richard's face she could tell he was impressed. "Would you care to join us?" he inquired, polite as always.

Jennifer extended her leg under the table to kick Richard into silence but he was out of her reach. Anyway, Flint was already consenting, pulling up a chair and sitting down, his own legs occupying the space between them under the table.

"I saw your article in *Financial Magazine*," Richard began. "Very impressive. Where do you think the electronic games business is going from here?"

It was Richard's attempt to make polite conversation, something Jennifer was usually grateful for, since making small talk was not her forte. But now his politeness galled her. Jennifer leaned back in disgust and sipped her Irish Cream on the rocks as Flint answered Richard's stream of questions.

Richard was obviously interested and impressed and she wanted to scream when he invited Flint to stay for another drink.

Finally, Flint turned the tables and began questioning the younger man. Jennifer continued to sip her drink, grateful for the alcohol's way of blurring reality into a more distant haze. It helped to block out the disconcerting gleam in Flint's eyes whenever they were directed at her— and the growing fear that any moment her lie would be revealed. Thinking about this, she took Richard's hand with a show of affection that he accepted with natural grace, squeezing her hand in return.

"I'm here from northern California," Richard was saying now. I've been doing research on the movements of prehistoric man in the area."

"So you're just visiting?" Flint inquired.

"Yes. I came to see Jennifer," he replied, turning to look at her and noticing for the first time the sparkling anger in her eyes and tight clench of her jaw as she glared at Flint.

"Why don't you tell Richard about how you managed to talk my uncle into selling you the ranch?" she said, stiff and barbed.

Understanding immediately crossed Richard's countenance, followed by irritation. "Oh, I see." He put an arm around Jennifer. "I was sorry to hear about the ranch. It's been a real shock to Jennifer."

Jennifer was glad for his arm and continued to hold his other hand, hoping this further suggestion of intimacy would make her lie more believable.

"Yes. I'm sorry she wasn't aware the ranch was for sale.

And I was hoping to have a chance to talk to her about it. But this doesn't seem to be the right time."

"No, it's not," Jennifer answered flatly. "And undoubtedly it never will be, Mr. Michaels. I plan to move out of the ranch in the next few days—so, you see, any discussion between us is pointless. Now I would appreciate it if you would excuse us. I want to go home."

At once Richard was attentive, obviously wanting to remove her from the awkward situation. He waved at the waiter for the check. "We'll go right away," he said, fishing in his pocket and removing some change. "I just have to make a phone call. I'll be right back. You'll excuse me?"

Jennifer could only nod as he rose and made his way toward the bar, waiting until he was out of sight before turning back to Flint. "What right have you to bother us like this?" she snapped.

Apparently unperturbed by the remark, Flint's green eyes sparkled. "It was meant as a friendly, peaceful gesture," he replied. "But you're surly as ever."

"I don't know what you expect. You ought to realize I have absolutely nothing to say to you. I can't imagine why you bothered to sit down and talk."

"I was curious to meet this boyfriend of yours," he answered. "I always like to assess the competition. Anyway, I think you'll be interested in what I'd like to discuss with you."

"Competition? Your arrogance is unbelievable. I would *never* have anything to do with you. And I doubt you could present any subject that I'd be interested in."

"No? What about the subject of Night Wind?"

"Night Wind? What does my filly have to do with this?"

Flint sampled his coffee before settling it on the saucer again. "The 'my' is exactly what I want to discuss. There is a certain contract that calls Night Wind's ownership into question."

With a horrible sinking in her stomach Jennifer realized what contract he was talking about. She had signed it nearly a year ago "for tax purposes," her uncle had said. It was an agreement to work for the ranch until December, showing Desert King in exchange for Night Wind. The contract was never supposed to be enforced or taken seriously. Everyone knew Night Wind had always been hers. But, as her uncle explained, the contract would allow the ranch to legally write off Night Wind's value as her salary and thus save a lot of money.

"But that was just meant as a formality, a write-off for tax purposes!" she protested.

"Perhaps. But my lawyer tells me it's completely legal and binding. It isn't December, the contract hasn't been fulfilled, and Night Wind isn't legally yours."

Jennifer squinted her eyes to narrow beacons of fury but his expression remained emotionless, his level look telling her he wasn't bluffing. He would take the filly from her, exactly as he threatened.

Straightening, she bit back a curse and said, "All right. We'll discuss it."

"Good. I'll meet you tonight at the ranch—without your boyfriend."

"Tonight!" she repeated, not believing his audacity.

"Yes. I'll meet you at the ranch at eleven o'clock. That's an hour from now and plenty of time to get rid of him."

Jennifer's fists clenched in her lap. "You mean you expect me to just have him take me home and leave. No. I'll meet with you, but another time."

Flint's face clouded. "Tonight, Jennifer." Now his voice was icy cold. "And you're not in a position to bargain. I have a buyer for Night Wind, and after paying the exorbitant price your uncle asked for the ranch, I can use the cash. It's up to you."

Richard appeared suddenly then, before she could answer. "Good-bye, Mr. Michaels," Richard said, shaking hands with Flint again, although his expression was stern now and his voice formal as he continued. "Maybe we'll see each other again."

"I'm sure . . ." Flint began, then looked directly down at Jennifer from over Richard's shoulder and finished, "I'll see you soon." Then he left with a final nod, his boots crushing down the thick brown carpeting with firm strides.

Jennifer's mind was in a whirl as Richard drove his Austin Healey back to the ranch. She wanted to tell him what Flint had said and ask for his advice. But she hesitated, recalling that Richard had been the one who had warned her most severely about signing that contract. Anyway, if she told him what had happened he would never leave her alone with Flint, and if Flint was thwarted he would probably go ahead and sell Night Wind.

She rubbed her temples to ease a tiny pain starting to build there.

"Headache?" Richard inquired.

"Yes," Jennifer said, seizing this as an excuse for not inviting him in. "I can't seem to believe what's happened. The ranch has been my life so long it just doesn't seem real that I have to give it up. I need some time alone to think."

"Yes. You've got a lot to think about. I only wish I was going to be here to help for the next month instead of at that dig in Oregon. I think you are going to need it."

"No. Not really," Jennifer said, in a braver tone than she felt. "I've been on my own a long time now. I can handle everything here. But call me when you get in. I'll leave my new number with my uncle or send it to your office."

"Sure. Of course I'll call." Then he looked at her more directly than before. "And Jennifer," he said carefully, slowing his speech to pick out just the right words. "To-night—the hand holding. That was just a show, wasn't it? Nothing has changed between us, has it?"

Jennifer smiled at the sweet concern in his face. "No," she said. "Nothing has changed. You are still my best friend. I should have explained before. I told Flint we were engaged to keep him at arm's length. I hope you don't mind."

"Oh," he said, then laughed softly. "I thought it was a show for his benefit, but I wasn't sure." His face turned serious then and he looked at her sharply. "You're certain you really dislike him so much? Once or twice there . . . well, I thought there might have been something between you two."

"There is definitely *nothing* between us." Jennifer answered firmly. "Mostly I just want to get away from the ranch. I'm going to start looking for another place first thing."

They drove into the driveway, past the guest house and on to the main house, where Richard pulled up the Austin under the thick oak trees standing in front of the large porch. Then, getting out, he let her out her side of the car and, taking the house key, unlocked the door.

"I hope you start feeling better soon," he said with concern. "And you're right to think it all over thoroughly before doing anything. If you need anything, leave a message at the museum and they'll be sure I get it."

"Yes. All right. I'll be sure to," she said. "But I know I'll be able to manage this."

"Okay," he said and, bending, kissed her on the cheek. "I'll call you tomorrow before I leave."

He waved then and walked to the car, starting it up and driving away.

Jennifer stepped inside then and shut the door behind her. She walked through the living room to the larger family room, where a low bar separated it from the kitchen. A note was there with her name clearly penned on the outside. She picked it up and read.

\* \* \*

Dear Jennifer,

Thank you for the use of the ranch house for the party last night. We'll be back in Santa Barbara next month, but I will be in touch with you before then. Let me know if you need any help getting resettled.

Love, Aunt Victoria

Jennifer bit her lip. She had hoped they would stay—had counted on her uncle's support against Flint. But now it looked like she'd have to do this alone.

She clenched the note in her hand. And Flint wasn't going to get her filly, she promised herself, straightening her shoulders. Everyone knew Night Wind was hers! There were witnesses!

She crossed her arms and shivered, realizing suddenly it was cold in the room. A fire had already been laid in the adobe brick fireplace at one end of the family room and, striking a long match, she lit it and watched it catch before stalking into the kitchen and opening cupboards. A drink? No. She needed one but she'd better have her head as clear as possible to deal with Flint. So, going to the stove, she put water on to boil in a copper teakettle and began assembling the other supplies for coffee brewing.

*I'll be firm,* she told herself. *I'll explain the exact situation to Flint. Surely he can be reasonable and, once he understands, he'll acknowledge my claim. But above all, I'm not going to act worried.*

Looking down then, she assessed her soft blue dress with its sexy low back, deciding immediately to change out of its vulnerable femininity into the security of jeans. She had just turned to start upstairs when she heard a firm knock on the door.

Flint! Well, too late. She couldn't leave him standing outside while she changed. Retracing her steps to the door, she swung it wide in a careless gesture that she hoped conveyed complete confidence.

61

He was wearing a plain blue shirt, dark boots, and jeans that hugged his small waist and athletic hips. An enigmatic expression masked his face, though she felt the power of a man who intended to win.

"Come in," she said coolly. "You're right on time."

He did, his casual strides falling in behind her as she led the way to the family room and indicated the green corduroy couches that faced each other in front of the fireplace.

"Make yourself comfortable—but not too comfortable," she added with a chilly glare as she headed into the kitchen. "I'm making coffee. Do you want a cup?"

"Coffee? That's some improvement at least. At the restaurant you seemed more inclined to give me the back of your hand."

Jennifer paused to stand in the doorway. "It's just as likely now," she said. "Except now I'm going to give you coffee first."

"So you're really so angry."

"Angry? I'm furious! How would you like to see fifteen years of effort being sold out from under you? And you might have at least said something instead of letting me show you around as if you were just a guest. You might have been honest." Her aquamarine eyes were large and dark and looked directly into his.

"I wasn't intending to buy the ranch when you were showing it to me, although your uncle had told me it was for sale. I made the decision after I left your room last night. Your uncle was getting desperate, although he kept it from you. I thought you might even be glad it was I who bought it and not someone else."

Jennifer's eyebrows raised. "And why would you imagine that?"

He came toward her until she had to raise her head high to keep her indignant gaze fixed on his knowing one.

"I thought I made that clear last night. And if you want

honesty, I think that unless I've misjudged you, you don't normally respond to a man the way you did to me."

Jennifer only stared, not knowing what to say since yes or no seemed equally bad.

"How I respond to anyone is none of your business," she said, turning her back and moving quickly to a kitchen cabinet, where she rummaged about for a coffee pot. "But if you're so intent on knowing what effect you have on me, then I can tell you I find you extremely irritating."

He sauntered to a chair and, sitting down, studied her across the low bar separating the two rooms. "And that's all?"

"Yes!"

"Now who's being dishonest? Or is this attitude your idea of being a liberated woman?"

"Liberated?" she said, slapping the filter holder on the coffee urn and shoving a filter in it. "I can't imagine you knowing *anything* about liberated women. They wouldn't appeal to a man like you, who prefers someone he can intimidate."

"No. I prefer truly liberated women, the kind who know what they want and don't mind saying it. What annoys me are the insincere ones who pretend and run away from the truth."

"And what *is* the truth as far as you're concerned?" she said, challenging him.

He tilted his head to one side. "Specifically, I think you feel the attraction between us, but you're afraid of it."

Jennifer refused to look at him as she poured boiling water through the coffee grounds, aware of the growing fury that gnawed at her composure, but determined not to let him force her into losing control.

"Look," she said, trying to stay calm. "This isn't getting us anywhere. You came over here tonight because there was some business about Night Wind. If we could just move directly on to that . . . I'm not interested in prolonging this any more than necessary," she said, concentrating on keeping her hands from shaking as she poured two mugs of coffee and set one on the low bar in front of him.

"Okay. I'll get to the point. I want you to fulfill your contract."

Jennifer stared. He couldn't be serious, and yet the sober lines of his face told her he was. "You mean work for you?" she said at last. "No! I'd never even consider it."

Flint's eyes riveted her for a moment. Then, unexpectedly, he was suddenly on his feet. "I see. Then I guess there's no point in wasting any more time."

"What are you doing?" Jennifer asked, following him as he moved toward the door.

"I'm going," he said, as if it were obvious.

"What do you mean 'going'? This is ridiculous. Did you come here actually expecting to hear any other answer?"

"Yes. Last night it seemed you wouldn't give up Night Wind so easily." He shrugged. "Sometimes I'm wrong." He started toward the door again.

"Give up Night Wind? I'm not giving her up. What are you talking about?" Jennifer said, following him across the living room and watching him slide his jacket up long arms and onto his large square shoulders. He was at the front door then and opening it wide when she continued.

"Wait! I have no intention of giving up Night Wind. What you don't seem to realize is that she is already mine and has been since she was foaled. My uncle and I made that contract so he could write the filly off the ranch taxes as my salary for showing Desert King. It was a formality. There was never any question that the filly was mine and there still isn't. Talk to my uncle if you don't believe me."

He remained standing in front of the door, although he took his hand off the knob. "I talked to your uncle two hours ago. He tells me the same story but agrees the contract is legally binding. And since he's already signed all the ranch stock over to me, if you want Night Wind, you'll have to show Desert King through December just like you'd have done if he hadn't been sold."

Jennifer walked past him and closed the door, leaning her back against it before saying, "You can't be serious. You don't expect me to work for you? I mean we would never get along. We would argue and . . ."

"No, we wouldn't. Not for long, anyway. I'm certain we'll work perfectly together, although you're going to have to improve your manners. I've been civil to you and I expect at least the same in return."

"Improve *my* manners! *You've* been nothing but impossibly forward ever since I met you."

A smile deepened the dimple grooves at the edges of his mouth so his face looked suddenly younger. "Possibly, but I've warned you I find you attractive. I'm not a monk after all, and you're over twenty-one, aren't you?"

"I'm twenty-five," she said defiantly.

"Then you're old enough to stop playing games."

"And what is *that* supposed to mean?"

"I think you know," he said, the flame in his eyes glimmering into hers.

"Damn you," she said. From the heat of her face she realized he had succeeded in making her blush. "As I've told you before, Mr. Michaels, I'm already engaged, a fact I take seriously even if *you* don't. Obviously, you intend to use your advantage over me to force us into a professional relationship. But don't make the mistake of thinking there can be anything else between us. You may as well give up!"

Her rage, her words, seemed to have no effect. He still faced her calmly as he said, "Possibly if you were married I'd consider it. But fortunately you are only engaged to that youngster. . . . What was his name?"

"Richard," Jennifer supplied, before biting her tongue and adding, "But he isn't a 'youngster'!"

"Yes, Richard. Anyone can see you're not in love with him."

"My feelings are my own business," she snapped, angrier still that Flint had not been fooled.

"But I'm making them mine."

He stepped closer then, so again she had to tilt her chin up higher to remain glaring into his face. And she felt even smaller than before when suddenly her view was blocked by the broad width of his shoulders. "You have no right to buy the ranch out from under me and then expect me to work for you as if everything were the same as before. It isn't fair!" she raged, wanting to somehow keep him at bay.

"It *is* fair!" he said, laughing softly, dangerously, and leaning closer. "Haven't you ever heard that *all* is fair in love and war?"

Jennifer crossed her arms over her breasts and shifted her weight to lean back harder against the door. "That's ridiculous," she accused. "You're not in love."

He smiled again, white teeth bright against his dark tan and, before she could resist, he had taken her hands, putting them over his shoulders before lifting her away from the door and into his arms. His rugged features hovered over hers then, as he searched the depths of her upturned eyes for a timeless interlude before whispering, "In that case you can call *this* war." Slowly then his mouth came down on hers, his surrounding strength preventing any escape as for a long breathless moment his lips touched and caressed and opened hers to receive his burning kiss.

She didn't want to respond, to feel these hot waves that swept over her in an electrifying current and gathered in circles of whirling burning intensity at her breasts and abdomen. Even as she tried to deny her response, her answering flesh grew frighteningly aware of each place his long solid body pressed against her softer one.

His lips drew away then, traveling down her throat in gentle nibbles, then harder, pausing at the vee that pulsed with the wild churning of her heart. "Stop this!" she said. But there was surrender in her tone and it didn't stop the hand that slid slowly down her spine, caressing her skin, revealed by the low back of her dress, and finally pressing at its base so her hips were drawn up tight against his thigh, firing a series of pulsating sensations through her. Without volition, she emitted a low moan from deep in her throat.

Her lips remained open as he drew slowly away and his arms relaxed their hold. It was like emerging from under water to open her eyes and see the lights, the room, and slowly remember the anger she felt toward this man.

Jerking herself out of his arms, she pulled away and stood in the middle of the room so one of the large chairs was between them. "And what was that supposed to prove?" she asked, wishing her voice sounded steadier.

"Prove? Nothing, maybe—it's up to you. But you're a fool to consider marrying Richard when you can respond to another man like that."

She turned away. "I didn't respond. You forced me to . . . to kiss you, that's all!"

Dizzy, her heart hammering, she wondered suddenly if he would make his point by kissing her again. She stiffened in preparation but he made no move to take her in his arms and only said, "Like I told you, Jennifer, it's up to you. Sleep well. I'll see you in the morning."

And before she could reply the door was opened and closed behind him with a click.

# CHAPTER FOUR

*He isn't getting away with this!* Jennifer thought the next morning as she looked out her bedroom window to find it foggy, a fine drizzle turning everything damp.

She had hardly slept the night before, alternating instead between cursing Flint in low murmurs and reliving the sensuality she experienced whenever she thought of the way he had kissed her.

Charm and money. He thought they would get him anything. Certainly he had succeeded in procuring Casa Contenta, but he was wrong, dead wrong, if he thought he could bully her this way. And just wait, she told herself, as she rummaged through her disorganized closet. After a few days he was going to wish he'd *never* forced *her* into *anything!*

Withdrawing baggy jeans, she slipped them on, belting them to her waist with a jerk, then she sorted through her shirts to find a green and yellow plaid one, which, her wardrobe mirrors told her, gave her complexion the glow of hepatitis.

So he thinks you're attractive, she told her image. What did he call you—irresistible?

She tested a stern expression in the mirror. Judging from what she knew of Flint's type this would probably be enough to turn him off. And even if it didn't, at least he wouldn't be able to flatter himself by imagining she had dressed to attract him.

She trotted downstairs, her boot heels making light thuds on the carpet runner, before crossing the family room to enter the kitchen.

The counters and appliances were arranged in a U shape, with an abundance of oak cupboards. The floor was tile, the walls a sober green, and a half-dozen copper kettles hung from brass hooks. The kitchen had a confident air, though she hardly set foot in it, limiting her culinary activities to instant breakfasts, scrambled eggs, and turkey club sandwiches.

Opening up the copper-tone refrigerator, she pulled out the milk and poured a portion in a tall glass. Then, tearing open a foil envelope of breakfast crystals (this morning it was chocolate), she poured them into it.

She stirred it haphazardly with a long spoon until the ingredients were thoroughly blended before drinking it slowly, aware in the tightness of her swallows that she felt oddly more nervous than it seemed she should. Mr. Flint Michaels thought he could control everything, but she could play tough, too. And he was asking for trouble by cornering her.

The drizzle had stopped and had been replaced by an even heavier fog, which obscured the guest house so it seemed a distant crouching creature as Jennifer headed for the barn.

Was Flint already there? He didn't seem like a man to waste time. She craned her neck to look through the fog, but the silver Jaguar seemed nowhere visible and, hoping she might avoid him altogether by coming this early, she continued on.

How many times, she wondered, had she walked this path? As she entered the big double doors, she paused, aware for perhaps the millionth time of the sweetness of the fresh oat hay stacked to the ceiling in the middle of the barn, of the pungent smell of manure, the soft welcoming nickers of the horses, all the sounds and smells that had signaled refuge since childhood.

*How would it be to go?* she asked herself. *How would it be never, never to see all this again?*

Her eyes cast about over the stalls with their double dutch doors, all hung with wooden signs carved with each horse's name. The walls between the doors were hung with pictures of Desert King as a colt, of Serena, and of the other horses, and beyond them in the tack room were the bridles and saddles she had touched every day of her life. Her hands opened and closed convulsively before she bit her lip, trying to control the emotion that caught in her throat. If Flint was here, somewhere, at least she didn't want him to see her cry. So, holding herself erect, she continued down the barn aisle into the tack room and removing a halter from a hook, approached Night Wind's stall.

The filly came to meet her, nudging her with the velvety softness of her nose as Jennifer entered the stall. Night Wind sniffed for any signs of a hidden carrot and finding none, began licking Jennifer's palms.

"Good girl," Jennifer crooned, touching the filly's nose and scratching her ears. "Good girl. It's going to be all right," she said, petting her. "We're still going to be together, you and I. No matter what, he won't take you away from me."

She stroked the filly with long firm pats, feeling her developing muscles, running a hand slowly down each leg and looking for any swelling that might indicate an injury. Only when she was satisfied that the filly was completely sound did she slip a halter over her chestnut muzzle and buckle it behind her ears.

Jennifer led her out of the stall and to the other end of the barn, talking to her all the way and stopping as they reached the large wide-flung doors. A rope was secured to the side of the barn and attaching the filly's halter to it,

70

Jennifer selected a black rubber currycomb from an assortment of brushes in a wooden box. She began grooming the filly in regular circular movements, loosening any dirt and dead hair, which she would brush out later.

Always she spoke gently to Night Wind and the filly responded by standing obediently—though Jennifer purposely appeared to be absorbed in her task, she was aware of footsteps approaching.

"*Buenos días,* Señorita. You come early."

Hearing Manuel's voice instead of Flint's, she relaxed into a smile as she looked up to find Manuel on the opposite side of Night Wind, the lines of his brown face forming an expression of gentle warmth. "Señor Michaels already told me," he said in a lower tone. "I am very sorry, Señorita," he continued, his wrinkled hand reaching to pat her upper arm. "I know what this ranch and these horses have meant to you."

His words, the sympathy in his voice and touch, all threatened to renew the sorrow she had suppressed. She had to swallow the tears that suddenly welled up in her eyes. "I'm going to be okay. It was a surprise, a shock, but . . . well, I'll get over it. I'm just going to have to learn to make my life without Casa Contenta." She raised her eyes to meet Manuel's. "What are you going to do?"

The old man shrugged. "Señor Michaels has asked me to stay, and this I will do," he said. "Casa Contenta is my home for thirty years. It is what I know. At my age a man does not have time to start over. *Comprende?*"

Jennifer nodded, patting the hand that was still squeezing her arm. "Yes. I do understand," she said, meaning it most sincerely. "In your place I would do the same thing."

"Has the Señor not asked you to stay?" Manuel asked.

"Yes," she said. "He's asked me. In fact, he's trying to force me." And seeing a frown come to Manuel's face, she related her conversation with Flint the night before.

Manuel whistled low between his teeth. "*Sí.* Yes, Señor

Michaels is a determined man," Manuel commented, picking up a second currycomb and beginning to work on the opposite side of Night Wind. "What are you going to do?" he asked.

"I haven't decided," she said. "But Night Wind belongs to me. And no one is taking her away."

The look on Jennifer's face was one Manuel had come to know as her determined look, and seeing this, he knew any objection would be useless, though he did warn, "You must be careful, I think, Señorita. I have lived long enough to know men, and this Señor Michaels is not one to anger."

Jennifer returned his gaze over the filly's back. "No, he isn't," she answered, "but neither am I."

Manuel opened his mouth to respond, but he closed it as they both heard footsteps coming up the barn aisle. They turned to find Flint making his way toward them, a disgusting air of ownership in his confident tread.

"Good morning," he said, nodding first to Manuel and then pausing to stand directly in front of Jennifer. He was wearing simple blue jeans and a light-blue work shirt with sleeves rolled up to reveal his tanned forearms, well shaped and covered with dark hair. His hands rested lazily on his hips. It was a casual pose. Yet the straightness of his posture, the wavy disarray of his hair, the way his boots were planted wide apart, all emitted an electricity, a subtle yet penetrating power that seemed able to either create or destroy everything around him at his whim.

Rationally, it seemed foolish to irritate this man, but the automatic fury Jennifer experienced, now that he stood before her, had nothing to do with rationality, and so she said, "For you it may be a good morning, Mr. Michaels. But to me it is the worst morning of my life, second only to two days ago, when we first met!"

She stared at him, refusing to even notice the warning roll of Manuel's eyes as Flint let the moments stretch out until the silence seemed loud. When he finally did speak, the deep note of his voice had an ominous ring. "I'd like to talk to you, Jennifer—alone."

Jennifer looked away, beginning to groom Night Wind again with an unconcerned air as she said, " 'Alone' is unnecessary, I'm sure. If you have something to say go ahead and say it." She continued brushing down Night Wind's legs as he watched her, and it would have infuriated her further to know Flint was having difficulty keeping a straight face.

Where had she gotten those clothes? And that hat—a disaster. Yet even so, Flint found himself affected by the line of her slender hips in the baggy jeans, the movements of her small wrists, the delicate line of her jaw. She was the only woman he knew who could wear such outrageous garb and still have more sex appeal than any ten starlets combined. And that she had undoubtedly dressed in such a fashion to discourage him . . . well, at least she didn't bore him.

He turned to Manuel then. "Would you excuse us? Miss Globe and I have some differences to iron out."

Manuel put his currycomb back. "Sí, Señor Michaels, I will be on the other side of the barn restacking the hay as you asked, Señor Michaels," he said glancing apologetically at Jennifer, letting her know he would be able to hear her call if she needed him.

Flint waited until he was gone before speaking. "It's a mistake to think you can hide from me behind Manuel," he said quietly. "You're going to have to learn to deal with me straight on."

"I have no problem dealing with you 'straight on,' " Jennifer answered, seeming to grow taller as she lifted her head to a queenly angle. "I would just rather not have to deal with you at all."

She couldn't believe his forwardness when he reached to touch her. Apparently he wasted no time in making a conquest when he wanted one, and Jennifer was left to wonder if all her nerve endings were located beneath the tip of his finger as he ran it up the buttons of the flannel shirt before taking the collar between thumb and fingers.

"What kind of clothes are these?"

Jennifer raised her eyebrows in mocking surprise. "You don't like them?"

"Is it possible to like something so unattractive?"

"Really, Mr. Michaels. I didn't know you would require certain dress of your employees."

His gaze was one of lazy humor, his hands never leaving his hips. "That's right," he said. "I'd forgotten you always have a sarcastic answer for everything."

"Oh. I'm sorry if I don't take your likes and dislikes seriously enough. But flattery is not a specialty of mine."

She had thought to avoid his touching her, should he try, but when he reached out and took her arm, it was a lightning move she couldn't elude. And it was useless to struggle as he escorted her out of the barn to a knoll that overlooked the house on one side and a rolling green pasture dotted with oak trees on the other.

She stood beside him, trying to concentrate on anything except the warm energy they exchanged where he held her, yet wondering if he could feel her trembling.

"Let go of me," she said, pulling away with a jerk. "And don't touch me again. Do you understand?" she said, trying to keep her tone even.

"What's the matter? Are you afraid I'm trying to seduce you?" he laughed. "Well, you're wrong. I want something far more than that. But you have made it clear you don't like me."

"Good," she said. "I intended not to mince any words."

"You haven't," he said, but he didn't look put-off. Instead his expression was calm, as if he felt he had the conversation well in hand, and it was this apparent confidence that made her add, "I'm sure women don't turn you down often, but with me you'll just have to get used to it."

"No, I don't usually get 'turned down,' as you put it," he said without pride in the fact. "But I haven't even asked *you* for anything."

"No. So far you've just taken."

"Yes," he agreed, "maybe I have. So now what do you want—my head on a platter? No, Jennifer Globe, right now you're not at all sure what you want."

"Really? What about you, Mr. Michaels? Are you so sure what you're getting is what you wanted?"

His eyes glowed a darker color as he looked directly into hers. "I know exactly what I'm getting."

"Do you?" she said, realizing too late she had involuntarily taken a short step backward. "Just to make sure, I should tell you that I wouldn't even try to win the championship if I didn't want it so much myself." She paused and took a breath, wanting to stop before she lost her temper—she didn't want him to be able to simply dismiss her as hysterical. Collecting herself, she went on. "Look, Flint, you've forced me into putting up with you, but we don't like each other. Let's just accept that and try to stay out of each other's way."

He raised one foot to rest on a barrel, leaning a forearm on his propped-up knee. "But I thought I've already made clear I *don't* accept that." His apparent patience perturbed her more than ever as he continued, "And you can stand here and fight, but that won't change anything."

"I don't know what you're talking about."

"Do I have to call you a liar?"

"Is that what you think? You think because you can kiss me and I respond that it means something," she said recklessly. "Well, I've kissed plenty of men and liked it. You're no different than any other." She looked for a glimmer in his eyes to tell her she had succeeded in penetrating his maddening calm. But there was a shield over

75

his emotions that told her nothing as he responded, saying, "Really? I don't think so, Jennifer. You may have a great deal of experience in some ways, but I would doubt if too much of it has been with men."

"Enough of it has been."

"Yes—maybe that's the point." His green eyes narrowed to sparkling emerald slits that evaluated her. "If I had to guess, I would say any man who touches something important in you. I suppose I'll just have to hope that soon you'll decide to stop hating and begin letting yourself be a woman again."

"You don't know anything about me or my past!" she sputtered, jolted that he had guessed so much. She was doubly annoyed as she realized that he had been carefully watching her reaction to his last remark and that her too quick and powerful denial had only made him more sure of his opinion.

"Just leave me alone. There isn't you or anyone else who can change me!"

She turned away then and stalked back into the barn where, thankfully, he didn't follow. And later, by the time Manuel appeared again, she felt able to control herself enough so the thoughts chasing about in her mind were at least not obvious on her face.

Maybe it was legal for him to buy the ranch—even to try and make her ride for him. Maybe that's part of being a good businessman, she thought. But he still had no right to interfere in her life like some barbaric prince who could command not only her presence but her likes and dislikes. He had no right to question her, to demand anything. As she stood there a plan occurred to her, a desperate plan, even a foolish one, considering what she already knew of Flint Michaels. But at the moment anything, even such a risk, seemed better than accepting his dominance. And rolling the plan around her head, her jaw firmed. *Just wait,*

*Flint Michaels,* she thought. *By tomorrow we'll see* who *has the upper hand.*

That night, the large clock over the fireplace had just struck midnight when she came downstairs dressed in a dark shirt, with her long hair stuffed in a cap. Once outside, she ran lightly to the barn. Peering toward Flint's *casita* she saw lights peeping from among the boughs of great oaks in the distance. It was dangerous to cross a man like Flint. And he was there, she had heard him drive in some time before, but the guest house was a long ways from the barn, and if she was careful . . .

The air was damp with fog that made the fine hairs around her face cling to her skin. She brushed them away as she entered the barn, then went directly to the tack room, where the keys to the truck were hung on a nail.

Hooking up the trailer was the riskiest part of the process, since the truck would have to be started and any sound echoed loud on such foggy nights. So when she stepped up into the cab she didn't even close the door but let it remain ajar as she started the motor, pressing down on the gas only as much as she had to to keep it going and let it warm up. Then, putting it in reverse, she backed up, fitting the truck's ball under the hitch with sure expertise.

She cut the motor and stepped out, still not closing the door. Then, moving to the hitch, she rapidly turned the lever on the trailer so it was let down easily over the ball and fastened down.

She hooked up the lights and brakes and the emergency chain, not even requiring the flashlight she held between her knees. Then, turning the light off altogether, she ran again for the barn, going to the tack room and removing Night Wind's halter.

The sound of footsteps against the gravel path startled her. Flint! Hastily she snapped off her flashlight and held her breath. Crouching behind the tackroom door, she took hold of a shovel and held it in front of her.

"Señorita Jennifer—*Madre de Dios,* it is me." It was Manuel, a baseball bat in his hand, his eyes round as they fixed on the shovel.

Jennifer almost laughed with relief, looking at the shovel and wondering if she could have used it on Flint after all. "Manuel," she whispered. "What are you doing here?"

"I hear the truck start. I see it was not Señor Michaels." One of the old man's eyes squinted and looked at her clothes as if noticing them for the first time. "What are these you are wearing? Why are you afraid?"

He flipped on the barn lights then, and she quickly flipped them off, keeping her hand over the switch. "Don't do that! I don't want *him* to know."

His eyes continued to narrow, confirmed in its assessment there was something amiss, an expression familiar to Jennifer ever since, when she was eight years old, he'd caught her hiding in the barn, playing hooky.

"Don't look at me like that, Manuel. I know what I'm doing."

"*Sí.* Perhaps. But why then are you hiding in the dark?" he asked, never changing his expression of disapproval.

"I've thought it over," she began. "Maybe Flint has bought this ranch legally, but he didn't buy Night Wind too. And as long as she's here on the ranch and under his control, I have no choice but to fulfill the contract. So I'm taking her away tonight. With her off the ranch I'll be in a better bargaining position."

Manuel stared at her before gesturing uneasily with his hands. "No, Señorita, this man will not be so easy. Señor Flint will find you. Today you make him a little angry I think. But you do this, *Diablos!* It is like waving a red shirt in front of a bull."

"Well you can't expect me to just let him have the upper

hand like this," Jennifer argued. "I won't be used. Anyway," she paused, hands on hips, "how did you know I made him angry this afternoon? Why were you eavesdropping on a conversation that was none of your business?"

The old man's stare wavered and his weight eased from one foot to the other. "A man does not need good ears to hear when you speak to the Señor."

Now it was Jennifer's turn to look somewhat abashed. She straightened, setting the shovel down. "I was angry and I raise my voice when I'm angry. He is trying to manipulate me by using this contract. Don't you see I have to take Night Wind off the ranch?" Her voice softened and she let the shovel down. "*Por favor* . . . Surely you understand?"

At the high-pitched, pleading tone, which she had used with Manuel at critical times since childhood, he wavered, shifting from foot to foot. Then, with a helpless lifting of his hands, he said, "Okay. But I am *loco* for helping when I think you only make things worse."

Jennifer smiled and squeezed his hand. "*Gracias,* Manuel. I knew you wouldn't let me down."

"Where are you taking the filly?" he asked, following her to Night Wind's stall, where the filly stood watching the proceedings with large-eyed curiosity gazing at them over the stall door, as if fully aware that the discussion concerned her.

"To Jeff Adam's place," she answered, opening the stall door and patting Night Wind's long, swanlike neck. "Good girl. Good," Jennifer said, slipping the halter over the filly's ears and tightening the buckle to fit the delicate structure of her head. Then, still talking to her softly, Jennifer led her back up the barn aisle and down to the back of the barn, where the trailer waited. With the uncanny ability of horses to sense fear in others, the filly seemed to know Jennifer was nervous and reacted to it, prancing on fine springy legs trying to put herself close to Jennifer.

Wordless now, Manuel fell in behind her, his attitude still disapproving even as he let down the heavy tail gate of the horse trailer so it became a ramp. Seeing it, the filly danced away, afraid of the cavelike appearance of the open trailer. But at a soothing word and a touch from Jennifer, she calmed and allowed herself to be led up the ramp, her hooves making hard hollow sounds, echoing in the dark, against the wood. Then both she and Manuel lifted the tail gate into place.

"I'll be back in an hour," Jennifer whispered.

Manuel looked stunned. "You are coming back and see him?"

"Yes. I'll need to bargain with him tomorrow."

Manuel shook his grey head. "*Diablos,*" he said, but Jennifer was already walking to the front of the truck and getting into the cab.

She had just started the motor and was pulling the door closed when the inside handle was snatched sharply out of her hand as someone flung it open. Forced off balance, she was unable to fight as she found herself scooped up and hurled the few yards to the barn side, where she was pinned up against it by a large hand encircling her throat.

She didn't, couldn't scream as his other hand pulled off her cap so her hair tumbled down in a shower of curling tendrils across her eyes. He only brushed it away angrily as he used her own flashlight to inspect her face. By his murderous expression Jennifer expected him to throttle her then and there. Anything was possible from this man, and staring hard into his eyes, she dared him to do it.

But he only stared back, his features turning to ice. "I guess I should have realized a promise wouldn't be a promise to you!" he said finally.

"Let go of me, damn you! And I didn't promise."

She tried vainly to push his hand away then fell back again with an exasperated gasp. "Damn you," she hissed. "I said let me go!"

80

He did, although she didn't dare move as he stood over her, his size, his intensity still pinning her to the wall as surely as his hand had a moment before. "In Texas horse stealing is a hanging offense. Fortunately for you, you're in California where there's only a jail sentence." He turned away from her then, his strides long and purposeful as he went to the trailer and lowered the ramp with one arm before backing Night Wind out.

His movements, his stance, all forbade her to protest, but seeing his hand so possessively on Night Wind's lead shank made her anger fresh again, so she said, "Night Wind is *not* your filly, Flint. And if I want to take her off the property it's not stealing."

He didn't respond, and she was forced to half walk, half trot after him as he led Night Wind back into the barn past Manuel, who stood back silent and repentant, the whites of his eyes apparent.

"I suppose that's why you were moving her at midnight?"

"It's none of your business when I do it. And anyway, what were you doing spying on me?"

He was putting the filly in her stall now, and this time he secured the bolt with a padlock from his pocket, which he closed around the handle with a biting snap.

She stared at it. "And what's that for?"

He walked away without answering, striding across the damp lawn toward the guest house—his house—never even looking back to see that she was hurrying after him.

"Flint, do you hear me?"

He did stop then, and he turned, his expression firm and completely serious. "I heard you, but I'm not listening."

"Well, you'd better listen—"

"No, you listen to me!" his words cut across hers. "Legally, Night Wind is *mine* whether *you* like it or not. I thought I could trust you, but it's obvious that neither you nor Manuel have any sense between you, so I'm locking

81

Night Wind up where you can't do anything stupid like taking her to Jeff Adam's ranch," he finished, the hint of drawl not softening the firm strength of his voice.

"What do you know about Jeff?"

"More than you, obviously. Enough not to want my filly there."

"What is *that* supposed to mean?"

He didn't answer, only continued to walk. Then over his shoulder he said, "And you can tell Manuel to pack his things. I won't have a man working for me that I can't trust."

At this statement Jennifer paled. "Manuel? Fire him? No, you can't."

She took three running strides to move in front of him and tried to stop him, but ended up walking backward as she looked into his face and said, "No! Manuel has lived here for thirty years. And anyway, he likes you. I was the one who talked him into helping me. It's not fair to blame him."

Flint stopped, looking directly at her as he asked. "Would you have someone working for you who would help steal your property?"

"But—"

"Just answer the question. Would you? Tell the truth."

"No . . ."

He straightened. "There we agree on something. That's a start, at least."

"But you can't just fire an old man like that."

Flint paused for a long considering moment, his green eyes flashing as they riveted her where she stood. "All right," he said at last, resting his hands on his hips. "I'll make a bargain with you. Your contract doesn't officially terminate until the end of December. But if you win the championship in November, I'll sign Night Wind over to you, and you can consider the contract fulfilled one month early."

"And if I lose?"

"Then you'll have to stay the extra time." There was a hint of amusement in his eyes as he explained. "I have to give you some incentive and getting away from me seems to be the strongest one available."

Jennifer's arms were crossed, her eyes distrusting slits in the glare of the barn light. "And you'll forget what just happened?"

"Yes—if you agree."

Jennifer paused, compressing her lips, as she considered his bargain. "Why do you want *me* to ride Desert King so badly?" she asked, thinking how well aware he must be that now, by using Manuel, he could force her into any bargain he chose. "With your kind of money you could hire anyone you wanted."

"Because you're the rider with the best chance of winning," he stated in a matter-of-fact tone that voided the compliment. "And I want to win, almost, but not quite, as much as I imagine you do." His eyes assessed her as if he already owned her and he took some pride in her prowess, "And having studied you, Jennifer Globe, I've concluded that you are a woman who has what it takes to win. I've heard it called a lot of things, but basically it amounts to skill and guts. That's what you have, Jennifer. And you're just the kind of person I like to stake my bets on."

"All right," she acknowledged. "So I win. What then? Surely you realize how much money there is in stud fees when you own a National Champion. Assuming I do win the championship, you'll be promoting Desert King as a prospective stud at horse shows and promotion parties, and you'll need a handler for that. So why are you offering to let me go early, when I still might help you?" she finished suspiciously, cocking her head. "You must realize that I would never trust an offer like this from someone as phony as you."

Flint frowned, his eyes showing the intensity of a man provoked, yet his voice was even as he answered. "Normally I wouldn't let anyone out of a contract early." A shadow of disappointment clouded his face as he continued. "But after this escapade of yours, I'm beginning to believe more than a month together would be longer than either of us could stand. Believe me, I wish you weren't the best rider for the job. I'd gladly hire anyone else rather than be saddled with your tricks and deceptions. If anyone is a 'phony,' Jennifer, it's you."

Stung, Jennifer flushed, but continued looking Flint square in the eye as she said, "And I can assure you, *Mr. Michaels*, most sincerely, that if I were free to work for *anyone* else, I would!"

She wanted to make that her last word, and she imagined spinning on her heel and heading toward the house, but something in his face—a light flashing in the depths of his eyes—wouldn't let her. If she didn't agree, he would sell Night Wind—out of principle, if nothing else. She had been worse than rude to him—though of course he had deserved it. But she suddenly realized she had pushed this big man too far, and having given vent to some of her anger, a cooler judgment now prevailed.

It would be stupid to pit herself against a man who held all the aces, at least right now. Oh, she would pay him back later, and she knew him well enough now to be immune to his dubious charms. Her mind made up, she abruptly held out her hand. "Okay, Mr. Michaels," she agreed. "You've got yourself a deal."

Their hands meshed and once again she had underestimated the effect of his touch. Immediately she drew her hand away, feeling his eyes on her even before he said, "You make quite a burglar in that outfit," his tone challenging her in a very personal way. And feeling him advancing, she took the offensive, lifting her chin to say, "By the way, you haven't told me why you were spying on me."

"I wasn't spying," he said. "I was looking for you."

That information made Jennifer realize for the first time that he was dressed in clean slacks and shirt and looked freshly combed and shaven. "You mean you came to my house?" she asked, aware to a fuller extent what it meant to have him living less than a hundred yards away. He could come to see her anytime. And there was no one to separate them, except for Manuel, who preferred to keep his own company most evenings.

"Yes—and my house very soon. I guess for right now we could consider it *our* house. But in any case, tonight I wanted to see how you were doing, but you weren't there. I heard the truck start and came here."

They were nearing the guest house; suddenly aware of that, Jennifer stopped, not wanting to go further. He stopped too and suddenly was closer than before as for too long a moment they stood silent in the dim light cast by a high pearly moon against a violet sky. Then his hand reached to caress her cheek. "I do care what you're feeling, Jennifer, even if I might appear harsh or even phony to you. I admired this ranch from the moment I drove up the driveway with your uncle, and I wanted it. But because I admire it, I realize more fully what this must be like for you. I didn't do this to make you unhappy. I wanted to make it as easy for you as possible. I guess I've been too hard on you. Maybe I'm so used to having what I want I've learned to expect it automatically."

The smell of his shaving soap filled her nose and she felt again as if he was surrounding her in that ring of his attraction. Why did he have to be kind suddenly, to speak so earnestly? And now the nearness of his large chest, the soft caressing note in his voice, all compelled her to yield to what might happen next. But when he leaned closer, it was a reflex action for her to put a hand against him,

85

pushing him away even as she tilted her head back, only to find his lips dangerously close. "Don't kiss me. Don't," she demanded, still pushing him away, her movements more frantic as they failed.

"I'm so sorry, Jennifer," he was whispering in her ear. "You've been hurt before, but I won't—"

"Don't say that! I'll never believe a man like you!"

He eased his hold and pulled away. She saw the disappointment in his face as he said, "A man like me? Who am I like—the idiot that did this to you?"

"I don't want to discuss this, Flint."

"Not now?"

"Not ever. It's my business why I feel this way, not yours," she concluded forcefully. She was surprised when he only said "I see," and didn't press her further. He held her away from him and continued, "Then let's call a simple truce. From now until further notice we'll have a platonic relationship, and if it's to be changed, then it will be because it's what *you* want."

"Fine," she said. "But I've told you before, Flint, you're not my type, and that's not going to change."

He nodded, with a smile. "You win." But even as he said it, the depth of his dimples, the look in his eyes told her she hadn't won—not yet.

# CHAPTER FIVE

If Jennifer had ever thought their truce would lessen the immediacy of the situation, she quickly discovered she was wrong as Flint appeared the next morning, looking perfectly natural in snug jeans and a work shirt as he supervised the stacking of a load of feed by several delivery men. She did her best to ignore him, giving him only a brief nod of recognition, no more than a queen might give a lesser subject, before going into the barn and getting a halter from the tack room to slip on Serena.

Perhaps it was her long association with the mare that made Serena so sensitive to her moods, for now the big brown eyes searched her face before the mare finally nuzzled her hand, her cheek, and then her hand again in a gentle comforting way as if she instinctively knew something was troubling her mistress.

Jennifer stroked the old mare. "You know I'm upset, don't you?" she said, marveling at the way horses could be more perceptive than humans. "It's okay. I'm going to get over this," she said, leading Serena out into the barn aisle and snapping her halter to the cross ties. She took a currycomb in one hand and a brush in the other, alternating their use on the mare's silvery dappled coat as she continued to speak to her in low tones.

Serena seemed comforted by the words and feel of the strokes, sighing with a rumbling sound of contentment from her wide sculptured nostrils. But in spite of Jennifer's apparent attention to the grooming, she was overwhelmingly aware of Flint when he appeared behind her at the opposite end of the barn.

How he had changed the atmosphere—had stamped it with a masculine vitality that made him the center of all activity. Before, she had been the one to whom problems were taken for resolution. But now Flint was controlling not only all she had commanded but, according to their bargain, now he even controlled her.

She continued grooming the horse, moving to the other side and refusing to look at Flint again as the unloading and stacking of the large feed sacks was completed and he remained standing in the doorway, his back to her as he looked out over his pastures. Flint widened his stance and took a deep breath, drinking in the smells of fresh air, grass, and the sweet scent of hay. He had been on the ranch only a few days, but the rat race of the city with its hustle of business, money management, and working from crisis to crisis already seemed out of another life and time. Suddenly he felt closer to the contentment of his Texas boyhood than he had been in years. It was as if the contamination of city life was slipping away from him and he was free again, living in wide open spaces and loving it.

Glancing across the farthest meadow, he imagined the new barn he would build, one to hold just breeding stallions, another, larger one for the new mares he would buy, and yet another place for visiting mares waiting to be bred. He would plant some pastures in grass, others in oat hay and alfalfa, and miles of fences would be repaired and repainted. By the time he was finished, it would be the best Arabian horse-breeding facility in the country. But first there were other matters to settle, he thought, shifting his attention to focus on Jennifer grooming Serena, and he smiled again at her baggy jeans and plaid boyish shirt. How many women had spent their last cent on finding just the right dress to wear for him? Yet this woman seemed to be making an equal effort in the opposite direction.

He walked slowly toward her—carefully, as if not to spook a wild creature, all the while studying the clean, pure line of her face in profile: the wide forehead, the short, straight nose, the full curve of her lower lip, the sculptured chin that held more than a trace of stubbornness. And when she bent over, the open vee of the shirt revealed the tops of her white breasts, held only by a wispy bra.

He looked away, not wanting her to look up and catch the destination of his stare, to glower at him with another of her "looks." But then, unable to resist the lure of her charms, he glanced again at the narrow opening and smooth white skin, wanting to touch her with an aching longing, wondering what she would look like without the shirt, or in fact without anything at all. And what might bring that smile to her lips, that loving one she used sometimes when speaking low to Night Wind, the same smile that touched him in a strange warm way whenever he thought of it.

"What do you want?" Her words broke into his reverie. She was standing up straight now, hands on hips, elbows pointed indignantly, booted feet planted aggressively.

He thought of telling her "you," of taking her in his arms then and there and leaving no doubt in her mind of exactly what he did want.

What was it about this woman? It was a question he had been trying to answer since meeting her. Of course she was beautiful—lithe yet curvaceous, as only such a tall girl could be. And she didn't even like him. There was novelty in that. Yet it seemed to Flint that it was not just this new experience of rejection that made her such a growing obsession. Many women had been rude to catch his notice. No, it was something different, something mysterious that made him suddenly willing to find a small reserve of patience, and so he said, "I came to watch. I'm interested in how Serena's doing."

"There isn't anything to watch. And Serena's doing fine," Jennifer snapped, wondering how long he had been watching her.

He came closer, reaching a hand to caress Serena's neck. Jennifer noticed the dark curling hairs on his knuckles, the well-shaped nails, the length of his fingers as he began to move his hand along the mare's shiny coat with infinitely more gentleness than he normally used with a horse, even lifting the gray mane and traveling slowly beneath it.

"Yes, she looks fine," he agreed. "When do you think she's going to foal?"

Jennifer shrugged. "I'm not sure of the date. She usually delivers about three hundred and thirty days from the time of breeding, but this year I don't know the exact date, since she was running loose with the stallion." Jennifer shrugged, aware suddenly that she felt self-conscious talking to him about horse breeding even though it was a subject she usually felt completely comfortable discussing. Hoping he would go away, she continued grooming the horse.

But he didn't go. Instead, he stood watching, seemingly aware of every move she made. *All right, let him watch,* she told herself. But as the minutes brought only a more intense awareness of his presence, she finally unsnapped Serena from the cross ties, put a long line on the mare's halter, and led her out of the barn and into an oval of white railed fence encircling a large area patched here and there with grass.

She kept her back to Flint as she led Serena inside the ring, then gently clucked her tongue against the roof of her mouth in a sound that made Serena move faster, away from her, and then circle around her on the end of the line some twenty feet away.

90

"Walk," Jennifer commanded, quiet and firm.

The mare extended her stride, her large belly slung low.

"Good girl. Good," Jennifer said.

The mare moved quietly around the circle to the right as Jennifer held the line in her right hand, turning her own body to continue facing the circling horse, a whip in her left hand that she held down so the tip sometimes touched the ground at her booted heels.

"Trot, Serena. Trot," Jennifer commanded. In spite of the heavy weight she carried, Serena perked up her ears and moved forward at a brisk trot, her feet snapping up in a sharp prance as she expanded herself with air and good health and stepped higher.

She seemed happy and Jennifer would have enjoyed watching the mare stretch her legs if Flint weren't standing at the edge of the ring, his arms crossed to lean casually on the top rail of the fence, his face unreadable.

He had probably come just to annoy her, Jennifer thought, to interfere, to even give her some kind of an order. She let Serena take several more long-strided turns, conscious of Flint's eyes before she stopped the mare with a sharp "whoa."

"I wish you wouldn't stand there watching," she said as the mare came to a stop.

He lifted his arms off the top rail. "No?"

"No." she snapped. "Lunging is a part of training and I don't like to have anyone watching me when I train."

"I see." He came through the gate toward her. "But I'm curious. How do you train a horse to do that?"

"I thought you grew up on a ranch in Texas," she challenged. "You must have seen a horse lunged before."

"Never," he admitted. "I've only had 'ranch' kinds of experiences with ranch kinds of horses. I don't know anything about training show horses, but since that's what we'll be doing I want you to teach me."

Jennifer's blue eyes hid all the surprise and distaste she

felt behind an impersonal stare. "Teaching you isn't in the bargain, Mr. Michaels. *We* won't be doing anything, and since I am contracted to be your horse trainer, I will lunge the horses myself—and without an audience, if you don't mind."

She hadn't really expected him to give in to her demand, and he didn't. Instead, he moved closer, patting Serena and saying, "But I might want to lunge my own horses sometime. It's good exercise and I won't always have you, will I?"

"No," she said decidedly. "You won't."

"Then you see," he said, hooking his fingers through his belt loops, "I do need to learn to lunge. You don't want to feel that you're leaving them in inexperienced hands."

On that count Jennifer knew he was right, and as she hesitated for a moment too long he took a step nearer and from behind her took the lunge line in his own right hand and her whip in his left.

At first she didn't release them, but finding herself captured between his arms and assaulted with the smell of his shaving soap mingling with the healthy odor of his male perspiration, she wanted only to escape him as his deep resonant voice whispered, near her ear, "Let me try."

Immediately she released the line and whip and ducked under one of his arms, then moved several steps away.

"As usual, you're not offering me any choice," she said, trying to hold her temper as she began. "Look. First of all, you should remember to hold the line in the same hand as the direction the horse is circling. If Serena is going to the right, as she is now, then you hold the line in your right hand, or if she is circling left, in the left hand. In the opposite hand you hold the whip, which acts as an extension of your arm to cue the horse to go faster or make her circle farther out from where you're standing."

"All right," he said, copying what she had demonstrated as best he could, with the uncertainty of a pupil. His look was almost boyish as he asked, "Like this?"

Jennifer sighed. Again he was managing to get his own way by undermining her emotional control. And already it was too late to object without creating another confrontation.

"Yes, that's, well, close enough. Now tell Serena 'walk.' And if she doesn't respond, urge her by shaking your whip."

"Walk," he said.

The mare responded, moving away from him and beginning to circle again, her head held firm by the line in Flint's hand.

"Good," Jennifer said impersonally after the mare had gone around twice, with Flint turning in place so he still faced the horse as it circled him.

"Good," she repeated. "Now tell her 'trot.' "

"Trot," he said.

The mare flicked an ear in Flint's direction, unsure because of the deeper pronunciation of the command.

"Shake your whip," Jennifer said.

Flint obeyed and the horse responded immediately, moving into a brisk trot and tossing her head happily at being allowed to further stretch her legs.

Flint held the line steadily in a hand that was neither too weak nor too dominating. The whip he gripped lightly but firmly. Already Jennifer could see he had the "feel" of it.

"Now tell her to canter," she said, and Flint repeated "Canter," smiling as the mare took the gait immediately.

The horse continued for several minutes. Then Jennifer said, "Now for the hard part, the 'reverse.' Let me take her for a moment."

Flint stopped the mare, handing Jennifer first the line and then the whip before stepping behind her out of her way and watching as she moved the mare out into a circle again, admiring Jennifer's excellent control. It seemed the horse and she were a single unit as Jennifer said "Reverse," changing hands with the whip and line in a smooth motion, while pulling Serena's head inside so that she turned and went in the opposite direction.

"Very good!" Flint said, applauding, his dimples deep. "Let me see that again."

Jennifer complied, reading the appreciation of her skill in his eyes, unable to resist its glow.

She repeated the maneuver several more times, then once again turned the line and whip over to him.

He headed the mare around him at a brisk trot. "Reverse," he said gently, pulling Serena's head in quickly, reeling in the line so she couldn't step on it, then letting it out again as the horse completed the turn and headed in the other direction.

In spite of herself, Jennifer was impressed with his quickness in learning the maneuver. And when he did it three more times, each better than the last, her own applause was spontaneous as he stopped Serena.

They both laughed with pleasure at the accomplishment. Jennifer was the first to stop, sobering abruptly at finding herself enjoying Flint's company. "I think that's enough for Serena," she said. Taking the mare, she walked her toward the barn, and when Flint fell in beside her she said, "You're a good pupil," in an impersonal way, hoping to regain the distance between them that she had felt evaporating only a moment before.

"Thank you," he said. "You're a good teacher."

She smiled now, a hint of challenge in her voice as they continued walking side by side. "But Night Wind and King aren't as easy as Serena to lunge. Serena will go around in a circle, providing you don't do anything too unusual. But the filly and King have their own ideas about which direction and how fast they'd like to go."

One of his eyebrows cocked upward and the hint of a

smile appeared on his lips. "Just like their mistress?" he asked.

Jennifer paused and looked at him squarely. "I don't think I have the market cornered on preferring my own way, Mr. Michaels."

She turned and started to walk back to the barn again, but a hand on her arm stopped her. Again she faced him as he said, "And by the way Jennifer. I want you to stop the 'Mr. Michaels.' The janitor at my office never called me Mr. Michaels. Why don't you call me Flint?"

"You know why."

"Yes. But we called a truce."

"And a truce includes calling you by your first name?"

"At least that."

It came to mind to ask what else their truce included, but he had stepped so close that again she was aware of the breadth of his towering shoulders, the very essence of his male power surrounding her, and she held back the dangerous words.

She swallowed. "All right—Flint," she said, moving immediately away from him and into the barn.

He stood by as she put Serena in her stall before turning her attention to King. The big stallion tossed his head eagerly as she entered his stall, so she soothed him with soft words as she slipped the leather around his nose and fastened it behind his ears. Then leading him outside, she handed the lunge line to Flint.

"You're going to let me go solo so soon?" he asked in a teasing tone.

Jennifer only nodded, knowing this move was prompted by a need to put some physical distance between them. But she could see that, whatever else she might think of Flint, he did have that special talent with horses—that rare sense of intimate communication that sprang up instantly between particular people and horses—an invisible link that connected them and that was far more important than the strength of the lead line. And as she watched him lunge King, giving him an instruction here and there, she saw nothing to shake her opinion. At first King was full of high spirits, and he reversed twice without being told to do so, just for the pure enjoyment of making a sharp quick turn and foiling his handler. But Flint was a match for the big animal, forcing King to a halt and turning him back to his former direction until King saw he couldn't get away with the ploy, and didn't try it again.

Having passed that test, Jennifer let him lunge Night Wind, and though the filly was more animated and playful, she took easily to Flint's commands. Jennifer suspected Night Wind actually enjoyed the workout more than usual, and she found herself annoyed. Everything was going his way—the ranch, Manuel, and now, damn it, even the horses liked him.

During each of the next three days, Jennifer rose extra early, attempting to avoid Flint while she worked the horses. But her efforts were always in vain, since he managed to rise just as early and further insisted she show him the basic techniques of training, forcing her to explain everything and suffer his constant presence.

She wanted to remain hostile to him. But she found it wearing to constantly be rude. She really didn't like conflict, and since he didn't attempt to provoke her, but instead accepted her off-hand treatment of him with politeness, she had no excuse but to be civil.

He continued to learn rapidly and, after a few days, she found he could lunge even the most difficult yearlings with apparent command and ease. He could ride well, easily keeping up when she tried to lose him during a mad dash across the open pastures, and he even learned to drive the two-wheeled cart with aplomb, though at first a spunky mare almost ran away with him before he calmed her with his firm hand.

Yes, he was quickly becoming an able trainer. And she . . . well, she couldn't help but admit he was physically attractive, particularly one day when she found him leaning against the barn, wearing only snug jeans that outlined his muscularly curved buttocks and black boots, one of which he kept propped on a low stool as he sharpened a blade down a long razor strap.

His jackets would never require shoulder pads, she observed, noting that his tanned shoulders were square and broad, the sculptured flesh round and smooth. His bare chest was a picture of power—a well-tuned machine that rippled with muscle to the belt of his pants.

How long had she been staring, she wondered suddenly, and she turned away, hoping he hadn't seen, telling herself not to look again. But she was like a moth drawn irresistibly to a light, and she couldn't help darting little glances toward him as she saddled Desert King, tightening and rechecking the bridle and girth and reins until it was impossible to delay further and she had to mount and ride away.

But that day all her concentration deserted her as she warmed King up over low obstacles before jumping him over higher ones. Her hands were unsteady, her legs unsure, her timing was off, and uncontrollably her eyes would slip again to the figure at the barn.

The next day was the same, and so was the next, until it became routine for them to handle the horses together. And as the leaves of the great oak trees turned gold and began to drop, and the days shortened and blended one into the other to become a week and then two, Jennifer found that in spite of her desire to ignore him, she was acutely aware of exactly where he was, even in the evenings as she sat reading or watching T.V. alone in the big house. Her ears seemed attuned to every sound that came from his casita, especially the sound of his Jaguar starting with the roar of a beast and droning down the gravel drive to a destination he never spoke of.

*He's probably going to visit one of his girl friends,* she thought to herself, glad she didn't care where he went. Certainly he never made any inquiries about how *she* spent her evenings. And yet, though he made no further overt advances as the days passed, some instinctive knowledge, something in the serious, pondering look in his eyes, the preciseness of his movements when he was with her, told her he was just as aware of her as she was of him. And it was possibly this that finally brought her to an almost painful level of self-consciousness and a sense of not being able to put him out of her mind. Finally, it took a near accident with King, when she inadvertently pulled him up over a jump just because Flint appeared unexpectedly, to make her realize something had to change. And at home alone in the big ranch house that night, she considered her alternatives.

She could simply practice when he wasn't around, she told herself. But already he had proved he could rise just as early as she, and he was always at the barn, always near. That was the problem, she told herself as she cursed into her pillow.

Or she could tell him the truth—well yes, and what was that? she asked herself. Could she possibly admit exactly what he had already told her with such overbearing certainty—that *he* did touch something important in her, something that frightened her, something that she was running away from?

She didn't know how long she tossed and turned, or when she must have slept, but she awakened near dawn when a gust of wind rattled her windows. To anyone who had lived in Southern California as long as Jennifer had, a "Santa Ana" was unmistakable from that first gust of hot east wind.

Along the California coast, the prevailing wind usually

came from the west. But a Santa Ana, so called for the desert canyon where the winds were thought to originate, occurred when the wind shifted and came suddenly from the desert at the east. These were hot dry winds that often pushed the thermometer up to over a hundred degrees and turned the humidity to near zero, so flowers shriveled in the bud and brush fires were fueled into infernos by the winds. The famous Los Angeles canyon fires were typical cases of such tragedies. Feeling the dryness of her lips, the electric crackling of her hair as she brushed it, Jennifer hurried to the barn.

In the few minutes it had taken her to dress and eat another envelope of packaged breakfast drink, the wind had gotten worse, and walking down the several steps outside, she squinted her eyes against the dust devils that swirled dead leaves into turning funnels that sped along until they were broken by the bushes around the house or the eucalyptus trees that were bending their tall trunks and swaying elastically.

Even the powerlines were blown, pulling taut between the poles, and as Jennifer stood watching helplessly, one set of powerlines frayed and snapped, falling to the ground, darting and sparking only a short distance from the hay and directly into the stall of Tazifa and her new filly. The filly now scampered about, whinnying frantically as she danced away from what must have seemed to be dangling, hissing snakes.

Flint and Jennifer were converging on the scene. Running from the other end of the barn, he reached Tazifa's stall just as she did and just as another gust of wind sent wires in the air sparking and hissing near the stacked hay.

No one needed to speak. All of them could see that the hay, if ignited, would turn the whole barn into a bonfire. Running to get a halter, Jennifer slipped it on a frightened Tazifa, then led her and her foal to safety. Then, throwing the halter on the tack room floor, she headed back to where Flint was moving the hay.

His shirtsleeves were rolled up above the elbows, and along his tanned forearms, muscles bulged in long cords that sprang into sight and disappeared. He dug hay hooks into each bale, lifted, then threw them to a safe distance from the wires.

"Stay back," he commanded as she approached. "A shock from that wire could kill you."

"I know," she said, keeping all the fear out of her voice. "But you need help."

"Damn it, woman," he said. "I told you to stay back."

"Why? Because this is a man's job?" she called back defiantly, having already taken up a second pair of hay hooks and started to hook the nearest bale. Then, using all the strength that her fear gave her, she moved it slowly, lifting only one end and dragging the other to pull it out of danger where Flint had put the others.

"Damn it, I told you no!" He had her by the waist suddenly, to carry her facedown like a child so she kicked as she went.

She refused to scream or kick or fight a battle she had no hope of winning. Then he was standing her upright, holding her by the shoulder, looking her in the eyes, and before she could speak he said, "I don't want anything to happen to you. I couldn't stand it."

Then he was gone, returning to the hay, and she was prevented from saying any of the things she felt when Manuel was suddenly there too, helping him with the last three bales, which they moved quickly.

Once they were at a safe distance Flint leaped into his jeep, heading down the road to the gray box which housed the ranch's hookup to the power line. It was a half mile away, but in several minutes the sparks ceased.

She leaned against the fence railing and brushed her hair back. The wind gusted harder, bringing tumbleweeds from where they grew in the fallow fields at the northeast end of the ranch and stacking them up against a fence like lacy snow drifts. Manuel was behind the barn where a eucalyptus had blown against it, and she was just going to help when he tugged hard to dislodge the tree and slipped, pulling it suddenly on top of him.

"Manuel!" she cried, seeing even before it fell that his leg was in danger.

Manuel's face twisted as he let out a moan and moved his torso convulsively against the agony before turning deadly gray. "Manuel," she repeated, trying to lift the log off the leg. "Hold on. I'll see if I can move it."

"It is too heavy," he gasped, "Call the Señor. He move it."

Jennifer didn't argue, and she had just turned to call Flint when he was suddenly there beside them, lifting the tree up off the old man and setting it aside. Supporting him with both arms, Jennifer moved Manuel to a sitting position. He reeled as if he would faint, though he made no sound.

Flint quickly examined the leg, his forehead furrowed with concern. "It's bad, broken in two places and one is a compound fracture. We need a hospital, but I'm going to splint that leg before we move him," he said, with no unnecessary emotion.

He wasted no time running into his house and coming out with two pillows, apparently from his bed, and two long leather belts. Then, putting a pillow on each side of the leg, he wrapped the belt around it, securing the injured leg between the two cushions.

Again Manuel was silent, though Jennifer saw him pale further whenever he had to move the leg. Then Flint lifted him, motioning her ahead of him with his chin, so she opened the door of the Jaguar, letting him slide Manuel in before she squeezed in beside him to share the black leather seat.

The drive to the hospital took place in silence. When Flint carried Manuel into the hospital the old man fainted.

"Does he have any family that ought to be notified? It's only a break, but it's bad. Maybe his family should know."

"He has one sister, Rosa. She never married, just like him. She lives in Placentia. I'll call her," Jennifer said, agreeing that Rosa should know, even though Manuel complained at his sister's smallest interference in his life.

"*Pobrecito,*" Rosa cooed hours later, leaning over Manuel as if he were a small child instead of a grown man.

Manuel, still groggy from the surgery needed to set his leg, looked up at Jennifer and Flint questioningly.

"Now, *hermano,*" Rosa said, the fondness in her voice matched by firmness. "You will come to my casa, *sí.* I take care of you. Last time when you were sick you would not come and almost died of an infection. This time is different. This time I take care of you." She smiled with a set of strong peasant teeth, the sincere smile of a good if overbearing woman.

Manuel spoke in Spanish so muddled that Jennifer couldn't understand him, though apparently Rosa could. "No, my brother," she said. "Do you think I will let anyone else nurse you, and you can do nothing for yourself? No, you will come with me."

Flint made a wry amused expression to Jennifer and indicated the door. She patted Manuel's arm and kissed his cheek before making her good-byes to Rosa, who promised to call and let her know how Manuel was doing. Then they left the two alone.

"He doesn't seem too happy to be in his sister's clutches," Flint said as they walked down the hall and out the exit.

"But they seem like loving clutches," Jennifer said as they located the Jaguar in the parking lot.

She was aware of her fatigue as she opened her own

door and got in, sitting back with her head against the headrest. Flint started the car, turning it out onto the street and picking up Highway 1 to drive back to the ranch. It was rush hour and the busy streets took all his attention. But Flint maneuvered the car like a skilled New York cabbie—tough, bluffing, quick to stop or start when the opportunity presented itself. Jennifer sat back, glad suddenly that his attention was drawn away as she slipped the *Concierto de Aranjuez* into the tape deck, then leaned back, listening to the Spanish guitar as she studied him covertly.

He wasn't really *that* good-looking, after all, she told herself. His mouth was too clear-cut for a man's, the sensual fullness of his lower lip taking away from his ruggedness. His eyes were too large, too long-lashed, his hair was the coarse kind with cowlicks scrambling it in every direction. His nose was nondescript. No, he wasn't that good-looking once you ignored the broad shoulders, and what difference did broad shoulders make anyway, or his commanding height? That only succeeded in making her feel smaller—not a good feeling. What did she really see in him? But she knew there was no single answer to that question, not something she could lay her hands on and therefore nothing she could easily dispel. It was like a chemical formula out of her control, like spontaneous combustion. But whatever it was, she told herself firmly, somehow she had to get over it.

# CHAPTER SIX

It took an hour to drive back to the ranch and by that time the winds had died down, leaving the air hot, dry, and very, very still.

Jennifer was glad when Flint pulled up in front of the main ranch house, and as the car stopped she opened the door. "I'll tell you what I hear from Rosa later," she said as she alighted. "See you tomorrow." She waved.

"Tomorrow won't be soon enough." He turned off the car and the engine died with a low growling sound and stood quiet, waiting.

"It will have to be," she said. "I'm tired. I need to get cleaned up."

"But what about dinner?" he asked. "You were planning on eating, weren't you?"

"Eating. Yes, something. There's really nothing in the house."

He was opening the car door and getting out. "Let me be the judge of that," he said. "I'm very good at improvising."

"Nothing added to nothing is still nothing," she said, knowing that her cupboard was in fact bare. "But if you want to look at what I have in the kitchen, you're welcome."

Jennifer led the way through the living room and into the kitchen, aware in a vague way of how the house changed when he entered it, as if his energy filled all the available space, altering the atmosphere completely. "You see," she said, opening the refrigerator door to reveal emptiness but for a carton of milk only barely cool, since the power had been off all day. "Nothing. I'll settle for another package of breakfast crystals, but I imagine you have more of an appetite than that."

Flint smiled as he considered telling her—or showing her—that his appetite included her. But he restrained himself, watching her carefully from behind an impersonal mask. Jennifer Globe was like a wild horse living free all its life and having never been gentled to halter, a horse whose experiences with men, he suspected, had been very painful.

Her aloofness had intrigued him initially, but he had never expected her to elude him so long, to bring him face to face with the most frustrating experience he had ever encountered with a woman. In all truthfulness, women didn't often deny him. And he knew that Jennifer was not so cold by nature. He had felt a passionate warmth in her, sensed a woman who would satisfy him as no other ever had.

"Don't you ever get hungry?" he asked without a trace of a second meaning as he closed the refrigerator door and looked back at her.

"Of course I do. I just don't keep anything too elaborate in the house."

"Elaborate? What you have here is an austerity program."

"Well—I never really learned to cook," she admitted, feeling slightly foolish, "so I don't keep anything around."

He frowned. "How about in the freezer?"

She led the way then to a porch at the back of the kitchen, where a long white freezer took one side of the wall. When she lifted the lid, trays of what had been ice cubes confronted them; now there was only water with dots of white ice floating on its surface. In one corner steaks were defrosting, along with chopped spinach whose green liquid was already oozing out of the cardboard box, and corn on the cob reposed in plastic sacks, all groceries left from her aunt and uncle's visit.

"These will do," he said, inserting big hands to pull them out.

"But we have no way of cooking," Jennifer said. "I like my meat rare, but there is a limit."

He laughed. "I think I can oblige you."

"But we don't have any power, no electricity for the stove."

Now he seemed surprised. He raised his eyebrows and laughed again. "You may be able to ride like a wild Indian, Jennifer, but with that attitude you'd never survive two days outside civilization. Have you forgotten about fire?"

"But we don't have a barbecue."

He only smiled that knowing smile and said, "Look, I'll take care of this, you go change your clothes."

For the first time, Jennifer took stock of her dirty jeans and torn shirt. There was mud on her sleeve and, for all she knew, on her face. Welcoming the excuse to leave and therefore not risk letting him see just how really ignorant she was in a kitchen, she agreed and went upstairs to change.

Within a half hour she had showered and dressed. All her baggy jeans were in the laundry, so her only choice was to slip into a pair of snug "dress" jeans that hugged her rounded bottom and a light T-shirt in pale lavender.

She gave herself an assessing look in the mirror, noting that the clothes did show off her figure, but tonight the fact that he might find her appealing no longer seemed as dangerous. Dismissing even these considerations, she waved at herself in the mirror. *Why should I care what he thinks of me?* she asked herself. *What really is important is that no one was killed today and the ranch is still intact.*

*I should be thinking about getting a simple meal and going to sleep early and not wondering what he might or might not think of me. In fact I should, if I can, treat him as casually as possible.*

But as she trotted back down the stairs minutes later she was aware again of the unfamiliar feeling of having "a man" in the house, not just any man, but Flint. She realized suddenly how impossible it was to be casual at all. He had changed everything; his presence seemed to fill every corner of the kitchen and family room, extending to where he stood in the backyard arranging a ring of large stones.

Already he had unwound wire coat hangers and had strung the chunks of meat next to potatoes that he must have found in the cupboards, and he had wrapped the corn in aluminum foil.

Obviously he wasn't kidding when he said he knew how to improvise. And apparently he could sense her presence, too, since when he looked up it was directly at her figure in the doorway.

"Do we have any wood smaller than these logs?" he asked, indicating the stack against the patio fence with a gesture of his hands.

"No. Those are the only logs here. There was some kindling behind the barn, but Manuel cleared it out last year because he thought it was a fire hazard."

"There's no choice, then," he said, coming forward.

The ax looked small in his hand as he took it from where it leaned against the fence before selecting a log and laying it on the ground. Holding the ax straight out, he measured the distance between himself and the top of the log. Then, assuming a wide stance, he brought the blade of the ax down to touch the intended point of impact lightly before raising the ax overhead.

Blue veins stood out on his arms and the long sinewy chords of muscle jerked hard into prominence as he remained poised for a moment. Then the ax came down with

107

blinding force, the blade hitting exactly where he had aimed, and with a tearing crack it split the log in two.

Flint straightened, letting the ax handle slide through his hand so that the blade rested against his fist, standing the split pieces on end, then, repeating the process to split them both again.

Jennifer had never considered herself either weak or helpless, but the sheer force of the man startled her. And with the ax in his hand, his muscles playing across his chest, he reminded her of some frontier cowboy completely capable of shaping the world to supply his needs.

Taking the chopped pieces, he arranged them in the ring on top of dry foxtails and grasses. Then, coddling a match, he lit it.

The wind had completely died down now and everything was still as the fire blazed upward, flames licking high for a time before settling down to coals that burned red but no longer blazed.

When they were glowing, Flint took the makeshift skewers and arranged them across the fire, setting the corn in the coals and ash on the outside edge of the fire.

For the next hour, then, the food cooked, filling the air with delightful fragrances as they sat together on an old bench Flint provided, watching the sun go down. Scrounging further, Flint found a bottle of wine in one of the back cupboards and had poured them each a glass, which they sipped while they waited in the gathering darkness.

Tired, but stimulated by the wine, Jennifer felt content. Somehow they started talking about ranching in Texas and he entertained her with anecdotes about his boyhood that made her laugh.

"You are a good storyteller," she said, after a bout of laughter he had inspired with a story about his first time on a horse. Their eyes sparkled as they exchanged a look that lasted too long, making Jennifer suddenly self-conscious, so that she straightened, pulling her long legs closer to her own body rather then letting them stray toward his.

He looked up, studying her quizzically, his green animal eyes seeming to ask, "Do you think you can get away? Do you think I will let you?"

She thought suddenly of getting up, of making her excuses and going into the house. But knowing how awkward that would be, she stayed where she was. Anyway, there was no need to panic, she assured herself. She could handle him. But wanting somehow to keep his hands busy, she asked, "And does an old cowboy like you know how to play a guitar?"

"All cowboys play guitars," his smile was white in the gathering darkness. "It keeps us company on those nights alone with just our horses and the moon."

"Good," she said, rising. "There's a moon out tonight." She indicated the nearly full moon rising on the horizon. "And there's a guitar in the house."

"Then I'll play, if that's what you'd like."

"I'd like," she said, rising and going into the house to retrieve the instrument. It was in her room, a relic from her adolescence. It was badly out of tune, but as Flint took it from her she was immediately aware he had more than a passable knowledge of the instrument. He strummed it with skill, tuning each of the strings in turn before asking what kind of music she was in the mood for.

"I don't know," she said, pleased she had diverted him and managed to put something between them. "You decide."

He strummed the instrument again, the strings singing before he began, his deep voice vibrating harmoniously with the strumming of his fingers.

So, my darling, I'm told you are leavin'
Don't forget me with your ice cold heart.

109

Please recall now and then how I've loved you
And that I never thought we'd part.

It had grown darker, dimmer, the sun setting in a glow
of rosy rays that shone on his face. And as he sang, his eyes
held that probing look that asked, that coaxed, that
reached inside and touched her heart, setting it beating.
She didn't hear the next verse, only the caressing tone of
his voice, which made her remember that they were alone.
Now not even Manuel was here to shield her.

"I don't like that song," she said, interrupting rudely.

The guitar twanged to silence and he looked at her a
moment; his thoughts remained a mystery, since he only
smiled and said, "Well, then, how about this one?" Again
he strummed the guitar before beginning.

From the Southland you grew to a beauty
Hair of gold, lips of rose, and teeth of pearl
But those jeans you're wearin' and that horse
You're spurrin' would never know that you're a girl.

The song continued about the misadventures of a tom-
boy whom everyone attempted, unsuccessfully, to turn
into a girl, and Jennifer couldn't help but laugh at the
funny lyrics, even knowing that they were, at least in part,
directed at her.

She was still laughing when the song ended and Flint
set down his guitar. But when he reached across her lap
to stir the fire, his hand balanced on her knee, and his
touch, the closeness of him, brought her laughter to a halt.
And when he straightened, his face rising to pause just
over hers, suddenly no one was laughing. Their lips were
hypnotically close, their breaths mingling, before slowly
his mouth was coming, was taking hers.

Oh, yes, she remembered his kiss, she thought, trying
not to be swept away by those lips that touched her with

softness, teasing, fitting perfectly with hers. And telling herself she would control his passion, she let him continue.

He wasn't demanding as she expected—he didn't force his tongue into her mouth, but waited, ripening her response, so when it did pass between her lips, she did not feel violated as she might have, but only sensed a languorous warmth traveling through her limbs so that they lost their rigidness and became pliant. And when his arms circled her waist and pulled her close, she didn't fight but let herself fold into the curves of his chest, her fingers lifting to settle lightly around his neck.

The kiss went deeper, searching the outer, the inner shape of her lips as they warmed to his, as they tasted his healthy, sweet moistness.

Her lips felt full, open, ravished, when he looked at her in the twilight. And it was something in those smoky green eyes, more than in his kiss, that made her suddenly pull away until his other hand caught her behind her neck, bringing her close, holding her firm, her lips so close she knew the warmth of his breath as he whispered, "Jennifer, don't go. I want to kiss you again, just kiss you, that's all."

The stern seriousness of his eyes, the hand still behind her neck, gentle but firm, the fact that he had kissed her before without things getting out of control, and an inexplicable need for him, all combined to make her tilt her mouth upward and slowly close her eyes as the arm around her waist drew her onto his lap.

His arms enfolded her, cradled her as no one ever had, lovingly, as if she were a small baby. Yet she could sense the strength of his passion boiling just beneath the surface, felt him controlling it as again his mouth came down to feast on hers. This time his tongue ran along the outside of her lips, slowly tracing the outline, then sucking on her lower lip, gently, as if she were candy.

It brought back another time—but Dirk had not been like this, so gentle, so respectful. Dirk had wasted little

111

time in going after the object he sought. No, Dirk's love-making had been far different, she told herself. But just the recollection of him was like a sudden splash of icy water that catapulted her upward from the chasm of desire into which she had been sinking, so she pulled more firmly against the hands that would have stopped her.

"All right. You've kissed me," she whispered. "I want . . . I want you to stop now."

Surprisingly, he did, the arm that had held her around the waist now helping her with a lift upward, so she was again sitting next to him.

"I won't hurt you," he said. "You're not afraid, are you?"

"Don't be ridiculous. I just think dinner is ready, and I'm hungry," she said, trying to hide the extent to which he had affected her and concentrating her attention on the vee of his shirt, which exposed the curling black hair of his chest, as she tried to realign her senses.

"Don't you think we should eat dinner now?" she finished.

She was surprised again when he only nodded, not try-ing to take the situation further. Instead, he went to check the skewers and corn.

His willingness to back off gave her new confidence, a sense of being more at ease than ever with him. She had expected force, but instead he had respected her wishes. Perhaps he wasn't so difficult after all.

With his broad back turned to her, Flint took the first skewer and emptied it onto a plate before cutting into a piece of meat to see if it was ready. Then sitting beside her again, he pressed a morsel onto the tines of a fork that he silently held toward her mouth.

She opened her lips and he set it carefully onto her tongue before her teeth locked it inside and he pulled the fork away.

He watched as she carefully rolled the morsel around

her mouth and pronounced it delicious. Then he tasted a bite of his own, never taking his eyes from her, as if it were she he was tasting as he savored the tidbit, and at last he nodded in agreement. "Very good."

He took the second skewer and emptied it onto her plate, unwrapping the corn and pouring on the butter he had been melting in a cream pitcher at the side of the fire.

They ate without speaking, their silence adding intensity to the moment. Jennifer could think of nothing to say to break it and only concentrated on conveying her food to her mouth, knowing that he was aware of each bite she took, that the movements of her mouth were heightening the sensual mood between them.

She had been hungry before, but now she finished everything automatically. Then, since she still refused to meet his gaze, there was nothing for her to do but look into the darkness at the almost perfect moon.

It was up to him to take the plate from her hands and set it aside. If only she was sure of what she wanted, she thought as the fire died down and one by one the crickets began to chirp until the air was filled with the urgency of their sharp mating cries. And when the tension had grown to an unbearable proportion, she began, "I want you to know that I'm not afraid of . . . of *this,* Flint," hearing a softness in her own voice that surprised even herself. "But it's impossible for me to . . . to get *involved,* I want you to know that." And maybe because of the wine she had consumed, or the fact that he still didn't speak, she continued. "I admit you are right—that there is *something* between us. But I want you to promise not to take advantage of that fact. What is between us can never result in anything but difficulty for both of us."

She would have moved away as she finished, but his hand took hers and his tone was gentle, caring, as he asked, "Why, Jennifer? Tell me what's wrong. You aren't going to lie about being engaged again, are you?"

113

She wanted to, but couldn't, and she only shook her head.

"There isn't anyone else, at least not now, is there?"

She shook her head again, wondering where this confession would take them. This was all wrong. Her defenses were crumbling. Maybe she had had too much wine.

"But there was someone else, wasn't there?"

She nodded. "Yes. But I don't want to talk about this, Flint. Not now. It's all in the past and long ago."

His hand took hers and pulled her close again, the warmth of his arm circling her waist. "It is in the past," he said. "And it has nothing to do with what can happen in the future. Relationships can be different."

But the meaning of his words seemed lost as he drew her even closer onto his lap. Suddenly it seemed that there was nowhere for her jeaned thighs to go but around his waist as he kissed her again, his mouth more urgent now than before.

He was unbuttoning her blouse and sliding his hand beneath it and upward as his lips traveled down her cheek to her jawline in feathery, fiery brushes that tickled her spine with a shivery desire. Her own hand rose to his chest, not able to pull away but caressing the black hair there. And when his hand rose to softly trace the satiny material of her bra where it shaped the underside of her breasts, before circling higher to the prominent nipples that pushed from the opposite side of the material, she felt everything inside her go soft, so her bones seemed liquid as his fingers traveled where no one had touched for so very long.

She couldn't have anticipated her own reaction—that she would go hot, then cold, then hot again, that her skin would tingle, and that a sensation would chase over her flesh, making her whole body tremble. Her nipples were erect, straining to meet the touch that explored, caressed one, then gently moved to the other that stood swollen hard and ready for his touch, and when it came the trembling started again.

This was too much . . . too much . . . How was it he could do such things to her with only a touch, only a kiss?

"Soft, so soft," he was saying against her ear, nibbling her lobe now before traveling down her neck, warming each place he paused with his lips that had grown hotter— or was it her skin that burned with its own desires everywhere he caressed? "You are so beautiful, Jennifer, so exquisite, I want to see you in the moonlight." Already his fingers had undone the last buttons of her blouse and were slipping it back off her arms, kissing her shoulders as they appeared, then the vee of her throat, then down, down to the valley between her breasts.

It seemed a barrier had been crossed that could not be regained as he undid her bra, freeing her breasts, so firm that they remained high and hard-nippled, thrusting toward the burning lips that took them with an eagerness suggesting the restraint he was using in not taking her then and there.

The intense maleness of him was overwhelming as he swept her into his arms before lying her down on the grass, still warm from the sun's rays. He was kneeling above her as he stripped his shirt, tossing it in the vicinity of her blouse. She had seen him with his sleeves rolled up, seen him shirtless at a distance, but she had never seen his naked magnificence so close and wasn't prepared for the impact of his perfection, the sculptured symmetry of his arms and chest muscles, the strong line of his neck that curved to become his collarbone, the breadth of his shoulders, the mat of chest hair growing thickest in the middle before fanning out over his chest then narrowing to a strip that ran down to his navel before disappearing into his jeans. She suddenly wanted to see the rest of him, to run her hands over his muscled hardness. His eyes sparkled in the moonlight as he leaned closer and whispered, "I want you, Jennifer," before kissing her again, harder this time, more demandingly as she felt his fingers undo her belt and unsnap the waistband of her jeans. Instinctively her hips tilted upward and she wanted to open herself to him but again rationality reasserted itself,

"Flint—please. I'm sorry, but things have . . . come too far." She was sitting up, or trying to, but he stopped her, kissing her again for a long moment before pulling away and whispering, "Don't fight me, or yourself. You want this as much as I do."

His voice was gentle in her ear, not demanding. It was like fighting the wind to battle her desire. Still she managed to say "I can't, I can't," even though her own voice was thick with longing.

She expected to see those green eyes flash with with the glitter of frustration, for his next words to be those of anger as she sat up, but this time he didn't stop her. Instead he was saying, "I want you, Jennifer." He took her hand and kissed it, the harder skin of his fingers brushing her palm. "But I promise I won't force anything."

He had turned her hand over, exposing the soft inner wrist. "Tonight will be just for you," he said, slipping off her sandals, his fingers massaging her arch.

The serious probing expression in his eyes compelled her to be silent as he set her foot down and moved down beside her, then above her, around her, his hands caressing, the black hair of his chest prickling her breasts as again his mouth traveled along her shoulders, then down her sides to the zipper of her jeans.

The jeans were tight and not easy to slip off. But he was kneeling again, taking them by the cuffs and pulling. Jennifer felt the roughness of the material as it slipped down her legs and over her feet and off the ends of her toes, to be tossed onto the growing pile of garments. Now only her lacy panties remained, and she felt exposed and vulnerable lying before him.

His gaze, hot and desiring, swept her and then he started over, taking one foot, then the other, kissing the top of it, then the arch, her calves, her inner knee, his teeth lightly taking the flesh of her thigh as a little groan escaped her.

"So you like a man with teeth, huh?" his laugh was soft and thrilling as he gently bit the other inner thigh, his arm reaching so his hand again caressed her breast.

Jennifer thought she would burst. The whirling inside her became a color wheel as she moaned again, unable to resist as now his hand slipped along the lower edge of the elastic surrounding the inner side of her left leg, then upward.

She was like a bomb ready to burst, a ripened fruit, a blossom opening to the sun. And with his first feather-light touch everything exploded with a thundering eruption so deep, so shattering, that it verged on ecstatic pain before shuddering, winding downward, and from somewhere deep within her throat came a last sound that told of all the delight, all the wonder that took her beyond time and knowing to a place of wonderful completeness where nothing mattered, nothing existed but the two of them.

It was several minutes before the filmy curtains fogging reality parted again and the wondrous after feeling disappeared, to leave her once again in cold reality. Slowly she rolled away from him, pulling her shirt over her breasts and picking up her jeans to slip them on.

"That can wait." His voice made her turn to find he had turned onto his back. "There's no one here, and it's a beautiful night." He indicated the violet sky as he leaned on one elbow. And stretching out a hand, he finished, "Come here."

Jennifer felt more awkward than ever before. As much as she had wanted the satisfaction he had just given her, she now wanted to get away from him.

"I'm sorry," she said, pulling on her jeans and closing

117

the zipper before pulling on her shirt. She wished she could have said this was all his fault. But in all honesty she knew that at the moment of decision she had wanted him. And worst of all, he knew this as well as she did.

"I don't want to stay any longer," she continued, knowing how ridiculous she must seem, though the churning emotions within her made it impossible to regain her composure. "I'm sorry," she repeated. "This should never have happened."

He sat up now. "Yes, it should have—and it will again."

The confidence in his face and her own sinking sense of realization that he was right drummed into her.

"I want you to back off, Flint," she said, faltering. "I just need some space, don't you understand?" Feeling unable to look at him any longer, she ran for the house.

Flint looked after her long after she had disappeared.

There was no simple way to explain what he felt, but he knew he had never been more frustrated by anyone than by Jennifer Globe. He felt caught in a whirlwind—while he had admired her from their first meeting, now she seemed to constantly occupy his thoughts. He didn't know how it had all begun and he certainly couldn't predict where it would lead. For the first time in his life of responsibility he felt a situation was out of his control. Not even their lovemaking had been able to melt the barriers she insisted on placing between them. It was enough to drive a man crazy.

He was still watching when the lights in her bedroom flipped on, and her shadow passed across the window as distant and remote as a ghost. Perhaps, he concluded, picking up his shirt and slipping it on, a change of tactics was in order.

# CHAPTER SEVEN

"You must be very proud of yourself, Jennifer."

"Proud?" Jennifer asked absently, not really listening to her cousin Lillian as she scanned the large living area that spilled out onto a wide redwood deck. Jeff Adams' house was large and it was difficult to find anyone among the many guests, yet Flint always stood out—there he was, talking with yet another woman whose eyes admiringly shone up into his.

"Proud?" she repeated. "I don't know what you mean, Lillian," Jennifer said, still observing Flint as he returned the smile of the small dimpled redhead. She wondered what they were saying.

It had been a week since the night under the moon, which she was rapidly coming to think of as *that* night, and since then—oddly, frustratingly—Flint had all but ignored her.

She had expected something different. Certainly he wasn't the type to give up easily. She had expected to be pursued and had firmly decided the following morning that the only way to prevent the situation from developing further was to ignore him as much as possible. But the wind had been taken from her sails, and she had felt all the more odd and impotent when he seemed perfectly willing to ignore her, making no excuses or even references to the night before.

And so it had been for the last week. He was always

polite, but he didn't try to involve her in conversation. On the contrary, his words were minimal. After several days Jennifer was left to wonder if he was just giving her the "space" to come to terms with the situation, or if he really had changed his mind about her being "irresistible."

Even worse, she was wakeful every night, as a war waged within her—between the passions that tingled through her body like the aftertremors of an earthquake and her practical voice that told her over and over that she should never have had anything to do with Flint Michaels from the beginning.

Then tonight, strangely, he had invited her to come with him to Jeff Adams' party, an invitation she had wanted to decline, but couldn't. And though she wore a pale blue off-the-shoulder chiffon that the admiring looks of other men had told her was flattering, Flint had given her no compliments. In fact, she'd seen almost nothing of him since their arrival, when one guest after another had cornered his attention, demonstrating just how popular he was already becoming with this usually "closed" horse crowd.

"I mean," Lillian was continuing with a knowing smile, "that you've done very well for yourself. How did you ever manage to arrange to be his 'trainer'?" She laughed. "I mean most women would pay *him*. Sometime you'll have to tell me about all those moonlit nights," she finished with an eager, lusty look behind her eyes, as if she expected Jennifer to confide the passionate details.

Jennifer sipped her wine to cover the discomfort she felt. Had Flint told Lillian something? No, that was ridiculous, she decided. He always kept his private affairs to himself. Lillian was only guessing. Yet Jennifer knew her denial didn't sound convincing as she said "There haven't been any 'moonlit nights.' Flint spends most of his nights somewhere else besides the ranch."

"Oh really? Where?" Lillian asked with interest.

Jennifer shrugged slim shoulders. "I don't know. Why don't you ask one of his girl friends? There are plenty of them here tonight."

"Oh, now you sound jealous," Lillian admonished, her eyes twinkling. "There's no need to be. No one will ever have Flint all to themselves. You shouldn't be so possessive."

"I'm quite the opposite of possessive," Jennifer said, goaded by Lillian's determination not to see her point.

"I hope I'm not interrupting anything, but I thought you each might like one of these." They turned to see Jeff Adams carrying a pineapple daiquiri in each hand.

"Jeffrey, aren't you sweet!" Lillian said, holding out a hand to take the tall frosty glass from the handsome young ranch owner.

"You don't mind if I join you?" he asked, and Jennifer realized he was speaking directly to her, letting her know with a swift practiced perusal and a smile that he liked her dress and was even more interested in what was beneath it.

Jennifer had never been able to deny Jeff was attractive with his blond wavy hair. Lillian had described him as a Nordic god, always prefacing it with the word "rich." But Jennifer had never shared Lillian's opinion of Jeff. He might be good-looking, but he was much too pampered and too forward for her taste.

"You know, Jennifer"—Jeff's face had lost the fixed cocktail party smile and had become serious—"I've been wondering . . . Now that Michaels has bought Casa Contenta, maybe you'd consider riding for me here at Woodmill Arabians?" Jeff took her arm and, ignoring Lillian, led her into an alcove sheltered by potted palms. "You know my stallion Argos will be jumping in the championships, too."

Jennifer was about to shake her head politely but firmly and edge back toward the crowd when she happened to glance up and see that her conversation with Jeff had drawn Flint's attention. Although the little redhead was still talking, Flint was eyeing her across the room and angling slightly for a better view.

So! He wasn't ignoring her completely, Jennifer thought before smiling at Jeff as she said, "What did you have in mind?"

Jeff's eyes grew bright and putting his arm around her waist, he squeezed her familiarly. "It's something we should discuss. I think we could come up with a satisfactory arrangement," he said. And she smiled as he continued, knowing that Flint had noticed that squeeze.

"As far as I'm concerned," Jeff said, "You can name your salary. If you rode Argos in the championship instead of King, I couldn't lose." Jeff's face was even brighter as he considered the possibility of winning.

Out of the corner of her eye Jennifer saw a figure approaching just as she said, "I don't know, Jeff. I'll have to consider—"

"What she means," Flint's voice interrupted, "is that she hasn't considered the future yet, although at the moment her contract with me will not be fulfilled until after the Nationals."

Jennifer stared. Giving Flint a taste of jealousy was one thing, having him speak for her was another.

Smiling brilliantly, she turned back to Jeff. "What Mr. Michaels means is that, while I haven't made any commitments at the moment, I'm willing to consider offers."

A flame leapt into Flint's eyes before a polite veneer covered it. He took her hand, then spoke again to Jeff. "But you'll have to wait to make any offers until after we've danced," he said.

The air crackled with tension between the two men.

Jeff frowned, moving a half-step forward as if to come between Jennifer and Flint. But something in Flint's face must have stopped him, since he retreated that same half-step as Flint took her by the waist and moved uncompromisingly toward the dance floor.

It was a grip she couldn't have broken without creating a scene, so she let him take her among the other couples, the power of his movements making her feel no larger than a puppet. Then he pulled her close, the length of his body hard against hers for several steps as the music began.

Jennifer had just opened her mouth to protest, but he was already twirling her away from him to the step of the swing beat as the voice of Dina Dawson blared.

> Turn my heart to stone. Dry all my tears
> You're the worst, worst man in the world
> for a girl like me who cares.

They did a series of moves apart, but as they came together she said, "I'll thank you to stay out of my business, Flint."

His expression did not show any reaction to the anger in her tone. "At the moment your business *is* my business," he said, moving her around him.

"My business is my own," she said. "And just remember your ownership of me ends in two weeks."

"Yes, I know." He swung her away from him again, still stepping easily to the beat as he smiled at her in a very approving way.

"Is this really the same woman I saw this morning in jeans?" he asked when they came together again.

"Don't change the subject. Why did you interfere?"

"Because I think you're angry enough to do something you might regret."

"I'm not angry. You're the one who's angry . . . you've ignored me all week."

He seemed to be unconcerned with her reply, and yet there was a new intensity in his gaze as he answered.

"I'm not angry, Jennifer."

123

She turned away. "After all that's happened, could you blame me for wanting to work for someone else?"

"Yes."

"Why?"

He smiled. "Because going to work for Jeff Adams would be like going from the frying pan into the fire."

Jennifer tilted her head higher to look into his face as he pulled her into a closer turn they did side by side. "I'm not sure I'm not already in the fire," she said.

He laughed. "You're not. I can assure you you've hardly begun—at least not yet."

"Not ever!" she said, wriggling out of his arms as they passed a side door where she could step outside.

He followed and was facing her when she paused, panting slightly from the exertion of the dance and from the annoyance of arguing with him. But as she regarded him, his playful expression reached toward her in its own irresistible way, so she fought down the feeling that he was touching her heart.

"Flint, old man! Good to see you." They both turned to see a man in his fifties, a short rotund man who looked dwarfish next to Flint as he clapped him on the back. "Baker told me you were going to be at this party and brought me along. Long time no see!" If the man had been at all aware of the look on Flint's face, he would have realized his intrusion. But he didn't notice and kept hold of Flint's arm as he spoke.

It was the opening Jennifer needed, and she took it. "Good-night, I'm going now," she said politely, counting on the man to keep hold of Flint long enough to escape. She moved out into the yard at once, then along the drive to where the cars were parked, glad now she had insisted on bringing her own jeep from the ranch.

It was only two miles back to where a sign hung over the driveway reading "Casa Contenta," a name that seemed to have grown more incongruous than ever, she

124

thought as she turned in, winding past Flint's casita to park near the main house.

The night was clear and unusually warm, and as she got out of the jeep the soft breeze that caressed her cheek was sweet with the smell of hay. Her thoughts still were tumultuous; knowing she couldn't sleep, she headed for the barn.

The leaves of the large oak trees trembled with the wind overhead as the gravel crunched beneath her feet. How many times, she wondered, had she walked this path to the barn as a child, trying to escape the unhappiness in the large hacienda? And yet how much more difficult her problems seemed now. At least then her choices were her own, but now her life had been invaded by an enemy she could not resist. It wasn't fair, wasn't rational that she should be fool enough to respond to Flint, when he was so much like Dirk.

She shook her head as if to clear it of him, and she was perhaps halfway down the barn aisle when she heard a low moan from Serena's stall. She stopped, and as she was retracing her steps to investigate, another deep, agonized moan drifted out.

Quickly Jennifer pulled back the bolt and opened the door to see Serena stretched out in the middle of her stall, her huge pregnant body and her gray coat making her resemble a beached whale.

The foal! It would be even earlier than she'd expected.

"Easy girl, easy," Jennifer said softly as Serena raised her neck with another groan of effort and reached out to nuzzle her mistress's hand. Her large brown eyes, usually so soft and loving, were now dulled with agony.

The sight sent a stab of feeling into Jennifer's stomach that dropped to her toes as she recalled Manuel's words on the subject of foaling. *A horse is born in twenty minutos, coming out like a diver with its head between its front legs. Any other way is trouble.*

If only Manuel were here now. Already she could tell by the lather on Serena's neck that the mare had labored far longer than twenty minutes and that she had "trouble." With a tightening in her stomach, Jennifer recalled other stories that horse breeders told only when they were supplied with enough liquor to blur the pain of retelling the experience—stories of mares that labored for days and finally hemorrhaged to death, foals maimed by inexperienced people trying to help, or breech births where both mare and foal died.

Jennifer walked to the mare's flanks, looking for some sign of the emerging foal, her heart falling and twisting in a knot as the mare labored with another contraction and still nothing happened. If Serena was to live, she must find help right away. So, stepping outside the stall, she ran to the small black telephone hanging in the tack room.

Scrawled on the wall beside the telephone were a multitude of numbers; locating the veterinarian's, she punched in the number and waited, taking a long breath and letting it out slowly. The phone rang and rang and she prayed someone would answer. Then, after what seemed an eternity, the line was picked up and she could tell immediately from the hollow tone that she'd reached an answering service.

"Drs. Howard and Morgan, can you hold the line, please?"

"I have an emergency—" But the click on the line told Jennifer that the operator had already put her on hold.

Again she took a long breath, letting it out slowly as, white knuckled, she gripped the receiver. It seemed an eternity before the line clicked again and the woman's voice came over the wire. "Drs. Howard and Morgan, can I help you?"

"Yes," Jennifer said, her voice urgent. "I must speak to the doctor immediately. I have a horse foaling and there seem to be complications."

"What is your name, please?" the operator asked.

"Jennifer Globe. I'm located at Casa Contenta . . . the Globe ranch. The doctor knows the way. He's been here before."

"I'm sorry, but neither doctor is available. You'll have to try later." Her voice was cold and businesslike, almost like a recording that had paused for Jennifer to answer.

"I can't wait. You have to understand, the mare is dying."

Still no reply.

"Listen. She's a very valuable animal. She's worth fifty thousand dollars," Jennifer said, hoping the value of the mare would impress the woman if nothing else would.

It did.

"I see. Dr. Morgan is out of town but if you could hang on a moment I'll try to locate Doctor Howard."

Again the operator clicked off and Jennifer could only wait, somehow knowing even before the operator came back on that it was hopeless. "I'm sorry, but I can't reach the Doctor. He is already out on a call where there is no telephone. I'm sorry I can't help you." A pause. "I suppose if things are too bad I've heard people shoot horses to put them out of their misery."

At that moment Jennifer's only thought was of shooting the insensitive operator, but instead she asked to leave a message, again stressing its urgency, and then hung up the phone.

She dialed Jeff's number next, frustrated to find it busy and remembering he often took his phone off the hook during parties. Apparently she was on her own. Taking a grip on herself, she headed back up the barn to Serena, who was even worse than before, her eyes clouded and glazed, her breathing labored. And for the first time Jennifer wondered what she would do if she had to put the mare out of her misery. It was an alien thought that would hardly register.

127

"Jennifer?"

The sound of her name startled her to her feet; though it was Flint's voice, it was suddenly more welcome than she had ever imagined it could be.

"Flint, it's Serena. She's foaling, but there's something wrong. I can't get a vet and the phone's busy at Jeff's."

Flint knelt beside Serena before running a hand over her mountainous belly and her neck and looking into her eyes. His face had lost all expression except frowning concern. Then, moving to her flanks, he pushed her tail aside and carefully examined her.

He didn't say a word, but Jennifer didn't need to be told it was serious when the mare contracted again, her rib cage seeming to cave in with effort, and still nothing happened.

"I don't know what to do," she said, controlling the edge of fear in her voice. "I've never had this happen."

Flint straightened, his face unruffled. "I'll need hot water, lubricant, towels, and some rubber gloves if you have them," he said, rolling up his sleeves. "There is a complication but I'm going to have to examine her to find out what it is."

His voice was as matter-of-fact as his look. Willing now to accept help from any source, Jennifer didn't say what she thought—that he had no more experience than she— but just hurried to the tack room and brought the things he needed.

Serena seemed even worse, if possible, when she returned a few minutes later. The mare hardly moved as Flint put gloves on his washed hands before beginning to do what he must obviously have done or seen done before, examine the position of the foal inside the mare.

Jennifer waited in tense silence, her eyes pinned on his face. After a time, a ghost of a smile played about his mouth.

"It's alive and kicking," he said. "And it's a filly, if I know anything about the females on this ranch," Flint added, with a larger smile that lacked the tightness of fear. "Now we just have to get that little gal born."

Next came a series of what Jennifer could only describe as pushes and pulls by Flint. They seemed once again to stimulate Serena's labor, since the mare groaned and another contraction came. Then suddenly Flint's hand withdrew, holding locked in his strong grip two front feet and a nose between them—a tiny black nose with a white snip on the end and elegant white stocking on the front feet all the way to the knees, where the black began.

It was a filly, as Flint had predicted, and a beautiful one. But as it lay motionless on the straw it seemed dead, its tiny rib cage caved in, its wet ears pinned flat, its eyes closed. But Flint still appeared to have the situation under control as he leaned to cover the baby's mouth and give it its first breath.

It seemed like a miracle as the lungs expanded to round its rib cage, and large brown eyes blinked open, looking at them as if wondering from where they had appeared. Then raising her neck, shiny wet with its long hair, the filly whinnied low to her mother.

The relief Jennifer experienced went clear to the pit of her stomach, and it seemed she could breathe again. Then a lump grew hard in her throat and tears welled in her eyes as, at the sound of her baby, Serena raised her own neck, stretching it to reach her daughter's nose in a first kiss.

For some time the filly lay in the straw, seeming to get her bearings. Then, as if prodded by an inner timetable, she began to scramble in a flurry of long, wet legs, trying to get up.

Long hoofed legs drummed the ground, becoming more coordinated every second as the filly came closer to lifting herself. Then she was able to get both front hooves on the ground, pausing a moment to catch her breath. Then, with another heave, she lifted, to finally stand on four feet that were splayed out but nevertheless under her.

She whinnied then, a sweet, gentle sound, before smacking her lips, her little pink tongue curling at the edges to try out this new sucking mechanism.

Flint laughed at the filly's new trick and, hearing the warmth of Flint's laughter, Jennifer raised her eyes to his profile as he remained looking at the foal. He might be someone who uses people, and he might have used unfair means to get her to work for him, but he did love horses; and he did, she decided, have an unusually strong profile. There was something about the angle of his chin, its broadness that wedged back to high cheekbones, his large eyes saving his face from harshness—and particularly now, when Flint's eyes shone on the foal with a special look. Something inside Jennifer stirred, and she looked quickly back to the foal.

"It seems to me, Flint Michaels, that you know a lot more about horses than you've said. Or is this another case of your 'improvising'?"

He turned to her with that same wonderful gentle light in his eyes, and she suddenly wished she had inspired that look, instead of the foal. He shrugged. "Living on a ranch in Texas taught me practical things about horses, but I never learned to show them the way you do. You've taught me more than I imagined," he said.

She couldn't meet the disturbing look in his eyes and when the foal nickered again Jennifer moved away from Flint to where the baby stood. The foal turned to look at her but in so doing lost its balance, wobbling first, then starting to fall.

Jennifer tried to support her, but the filly's weight was coming down hard on her when suddenly Flint was on the opposite side of the foal, pulling the bewildered baby upright again.

Their motions had been swift, and Jennifer's only thought was to keep the filly on her feet. But now as the filly stopped wobbling and her pink tongue reappeared, smacking comically and making Jennifer giggle, it became clear that Flint did not mean to remove the hand that now rested over hers on the filly's back.

Jennifer started to pull away, but he caught it. "It's good to see you laugh," he said. Jennifer looked away from the green eyes whose light seemed so soft, so temptingly warm. Her whole body, still taut from the tension of the filly's birth, wanted to lean against that broad chest.

"Help me," he said, moving the filly toward Serena, who now stood quietly. "This little one needs to nurse."

Jennifer helped the filly balance, wrapping her arms around her chest and rump as, with patient, practiced hands, Flint guided the baby's mouth to the mare's bag and two long teats.

It was only a short time until she was nursing happily, and Flint motioned Jennifer away from the foal to sit with him in the semidarkness.

The mare nuzzled her new baby affectionately as the filly sucked loud and strong. In the intimacy of the darkness, the new life before them, it seemed a moment for confidences as he took her hand and asked, "Are you still so eager to leave the ranch?"

"Of course," she said, throwing back her hair. But even as she said it she knew she didn't sound convincing. The hand holding hers was gently transferring warmth from his fingers to hers.

"I don't believe it," he said, yet the knuckle of his forefinger that traced her jaw line was not a challenge but a caress.

Jennifer tried to remember how angry she was. He used me, and he's still using me, *just* using me. But somehow the blazing fury she wanted to reexperience did not come.

131

"What are you doing, Flint?" she asked at last.

He laughed. "So you *can* call me by name. You don't do that very often, you know. You really avoid it. Why?"

"I asked my question first," she said.

"Yes. I guess you did. What was it? What am I doing?" He seemed to ponder. "I suppose you mean by that why am I here?"

"Yes."

"Well, I suppose it's because when you didn't come back to the party I noticed the jeep was gone, so I came back. When I saw the barn lights I thought you might be here. I never can seem to resist you. Call me a fool. Because I'm beginning to think I am one."

He touched her again, his fingers gently brushing the stray hairs around her face, then running along her shoulder and down her arm in a trail of fire.

"You a fool? You make fools out of other people, Flint. *You* are never the fool."

"No? Is that why I keep beating myself against these defenses of yours?"

"I doubt it," she said sarcastically. "Probably you've been trying so hard for the same reasons as most men. You can't be denied anything, and you prefer a challenge."

She could see by the look on his face that her words had succeeded in annoying him. But feeling suddenly as if he were cornering her, she got up and walked outside the stall.

She knew he would follow, and she had only gotten beyond the barn, where the unbaled hay was stacked, when he took her upper arm and whirled her around. "Stop running away, Jennifer," he said tightly. "I'm not some kind of monster trying to run a number on you. I merely want you to admit the obvious."

It was dark around them now, except for the brightness of a full moon and a twinkling of stars peeping among gray cloud shapes. And it was warm, too warm, Jennifer thought as she turned to face Flint, acutely aware of where he held her arm, his fingers touching the side of her breast, his touch causing her nipple to harden.

She wanted to pull away, but somehow her stubbornness, her pride, and this feeling that was roving her abdomen like a hungry beast would not let her move.

Still she tilted her chin up, braving him. "Getting me to admit the obvious. Is that what you thought you were doing the other night?"

"Yes, in a way. But I've known since we first met that we were physically attracted to each other. What I'm interested in now is what makes that intriguing mind of yours tick."

"Well, if it's obvious, why do I need to admit anything?" she said, wanting to run away from the light in his eyes that touched her in dangerous ways. She never wanted to be touched again. "I want to go back to the house," she whispered.

"No. Not yet, Jennifer. Later, but not now."

"I have to. This is no good," she said, aware of the compelling atmosphere building around her, of his arm sliding around her waist to draw her nearer, of her hardened nipples being pressed into his chest, of the low moan that she stifled in her throat.

"Why?" he was asking, his thumb touching the sensitive hollow beneath her ear.

She tried to push him away, but her arms felt weak, useless, as she said, "Because! Because it's all wrong. I don't want to feel this way . . . to care for . . ." She paused before she said any more, already sorry her tongue had run away with her. "Look," she began again. "I only know what my instincts say, and . . ."

He pulled her nearer, leaning his head to kiss the line of her chin, slowly savoring each inch of skin up to her ear, reducing her resistance further as her limbs felt suddenly as weak and unsteady as the newborn foal's.

"What do your instincts say?" he asked, his eyes probing into hers again.

"That I have no business being here. That I'm being ridiculous and foolish. And that I will pay for all this with a lot of pain."

He continued to hold her dangerously close, the strength of his arms bracing her as his fingers traced their way up her back to the back of her neck, touching the hair there, gently pulling it, then moving higher to where she had pinned it with a long silver clip.

She heard a click as he snapped it open, felt the hair that had been held taut against her head loosen into a heavy wave that fell onto her shoulders in silky strands.

He buried his face in the blond mass, as if it were a shower of water and he dying of thirst. "I don't know how to explain it," he said, pausing to formulate his words. "I understand investment strategies, how to motivate employees, even how to birth a horse. But as far as you're concerned, I've had to go on instinct, too, and my instincts say that no matter how much I see you I want to see more. Part of me—and God help me—feels, well, at peace with myself when I'm with you." He smiled. "Does that seem silly? But the truth is, I can't seem to get enough of you, Jennifer. I wish I understood why, but I don't."

If she turned her lips only slightly toward him they would touch his cheek. And if that happened there would be no going back. So she turned her face in the opposite direction, away from him, not wanting him to see her eyes.

He was closer, his voice deeper—nearer her ear. "Do you feel anything like that, Jennifer?"

She knew she felt an equally unexplainable need for him. And somehow now, after watching him deliver the filly, feeling his calm strength and finally sharing the marvel of the birth, everything she held against him seemed more clouded than ever. So she said nothing. And when she didn't answer the tightening of his body, the pulling away made her realize, even before he sighed long and windily, that she had disappointed him. "It's not an easy thing to put yourself on the line and be rejected," he said.

"I didn't reject you, not exactly," she said.

"Is that what you think?"

"Well. I do have certain feelings," she admitted.

He caressed a curl that had fallen over her breast. The touch held her mystified, unable to move even if his hand had not traveled up her neck to circle around its back and hold her pinned immobile.

"Feelings?" He smiled. "Well that's a start, anyway, something to work with." His hand worked up her throat to cup her chin. "And now I'm going to kiss you, Jennifer," he said, with a forcefulness behind his words that told her there was no escape. "Don't fight me, please," he finished in a whisper.

"It won't matter," she moaned. "You know you're stronger."

"I don't want to use my strength. I want you to want me," he said. "I know you think I'm difficult." His thumb touched her nose, her cheek, then her lips, which he brushed softly. "I am difficult," he admitted. "But I can be gentle too." He held her closer, grinding her into his body. "And now I'm going to show you."

His firm features were hovering over hers, and Jennifer knew her defenses were no match for the passion he evoked. Everything seemed to force her to do as he wished —as she wished, too, a voice within her admitted.

"The other night . . . it should never have happened," she whispered as his lips made a slow path down her neck and onto her shoulders.

He picked her up then, and she didn't resist as he carried her to where the hay was stacked like a giant golden nest, laying her there, his own body following her down,

135

his lips remaining close to hers and bearing an inevitability.

"It wouldn't have mattered," he said. "This still would have happened."

"Flint—Flint, I can't do this. You have to understand —"

"I do understand—better than you know." His eyes filled with an intensity of need she felt him trying to control. His lips lowered to pause only a breath away from hers as he whispered, "Come, Jennifer, kiss me."

"Flint." His name became both a protest and a caress. She turned her head, unable to resist him, her eyes becoming deeply blue as their lips joined and it seemed they melted one into the other.

Jennifer let her hands roam over the broad expanse of his back, measuring the width of his shoulders and then sliding downward to the taper of his waist, wanting this to go on forever but knowing it would not. And then she dared not think at all as his fingers took the zipper of her dress to slide slowly down, then pulled the dress off to reveal the gossamer bra, a strapless affair made of nothing but lace.

He whistled low between his teeth. "I knew it all the time. You really are a fairy princess." He smiled and his voice lowered. "At least that's what you look like to me." His lips took hers again as he continued to slide the dress down over her hips until she felt it fold around her ankles. Then gentle fingers took the clasp of her bra. She felt it loosen then and fall free from her, releasing her breasts to the roughened palms that stimulated the nipples to peaks.

Standing up, he removed his own clothes, dropping them onto a heap off the edge of their straw pedestal. Then he was kneeling above her, magnificent in his nakedness, his perfection silhouetted against the moon, and she knew she was quivering. Now he would make love to her, and the hot desire in her own fevered blood couldn't deny him.

His fingers were calloused, but his touch was admiring and slow as he traced her knee, then trailed along her thigh, which opened to his touch of its own accord.

*I want him,* she thought as he took her ankle lightly in hand, his finger and thumb meeting around the slimness, before sliding upward along her calf. *I want him and I can't fight it anymore.*

There was a coiling and uncoiling in her belly as he stroked the silken material of her bikini panties, tracing their outline, his fingers seeming to leave a path of fire that warmed her to a burning need.

"Flint," she whispered, hardly aware she spoke as the fire burned brighter.

His hands had taken opposite sides of her bikini panties and slowly he began to strip them from her body, his kisses following them down her thighs. Then he was parting her legs wider and kneeling between them. He was hard and ready and she couldn't resist reaching to touch him, watching his face register an added dimension of pleasure and desire as her hand closed around his hardness. His skin was so soft and, as he lowered, she guided him to the center of her need.

Her body was moist and hot, but he felt even hotter as he pressed against her, sending her on an urgent upward spiral. Still he waited, and she could feel the intensity of his passion from the slight trembling of his hands as they traveled along her waist and up to her breasts.

"Flint, Flint," she whispered again, hearing the ragged, primitive note in her own voice that invited him to take her.

"Do you want me now?"

"Yes, Flint! Yes, you know . . ." But the rest of her words became a sigh as in an easy movement and bursting of pleasure, they became one.

His body seemed to flex with every muscle, driving forward, then paused, suspended, before relaxing.

Moments passed as he remained still. Was it over? And a deep disappointment was flooding her and settling in when she saw the faint smile on his face. It teased her even before she realized that he was ready all over again, and she found herself returning his smile.

He took her face between his hands, talking to her, whispering soft words that she hardly heard but more felt in the care he took with her, the soaring spiral on which he carried her to peak after unknown peak of unimagined delight. Then she was falling, bursting with a deep, wrenching wonderfulness, moaning her pleasure into his mouth as he kissed her. Then sinking, sinking into a warm abyss of perfect contentment.

They lay clutched in each other's arms for a long leisurely time as the euphoria receded. Finally Jennifer could no longer keep from coming to earth. She wanted suddenly to cry, but forcibly held back the tears. He was kissing her cheeks then, before lifting off her with an easy press of his arms.

She felt vulnerable, completely ridiculous, in fact, here, naked. And somehow even the good, satisfying feeling inside her seemed suddenly the enemy too. And without wanting to she remembered lying naked in Dirk's arms like this—well, no, this was different. But still it was enough the same so she recalled, with a vivid stroke of pain in her chest, how it all had ended.

"Jennifer," he whispered, the tips of his fingers brushing her temples. She didn't answer as she looked up at him and felt a deep fathomless ache within her.

She reached for her dress, but he took her arm, lifting the hand and kissing it. "Don't," he said. "You have such a beautiful body."

She stared up at him. "But I'm cold," she said, wanting some excuse to escape from this total intimacy.

He only smiled. "We can fix that." And scooping her

138

into his arms, he held her gently as he walked around the end of the barn and toward the casita—his casita—his territory, she realized.

"Flint, I don't want to go . . . inside." And when he paid no attention she kicked her legs, pulling herself away from the broad width of his chest, away from his fatal charisma that threatened to swallow up her will.

"Flint, I want you to put me down."

They had gone through double iron gates to reach a small patio outside the adobe brick house, and now he did pause. It was one story, and beneath the wide overhang of tile roof the bedroom was visible through the window. A low light sent a glow over the bed, invitingly wide and thrown with an Indian rug. In all the days they had spent together she had never been to the casita or, as she had began to think of it, his lair.

"Jennifer. Come with me. Sleep beside me tonight," His lips touched her ear. "I want to wake up holding you."

She felt herself drawn toward him by a compelling sensation of surrender. He had made her feel as no one ever had. Why not spend the night with him? She wanted to. And yet, once inside with him she would lose all perspective, all will. She would be trapped.

"No, Flint." She pushed hard against him. "Not now . . . not tonight." And when she continued to push he did set her down, though he still gripped her upper arms as he held her gently away from him, his face sobering.

"I want you to stay, Jennifer."

"No. It's not the right time. Too much has happened already."

"Do you regret it?"

"Yes, part of me does."

"And the other part?"

She tried to pull away, but he prevented her still. "You're not answering me."

"You know I wanted you and you know it was good,"

she said fiercely between her teeth. "But that doesn't mean I want to spend the night with you."

There was a pause between them while Jennifer became even more acutely aware of her nakedness, and of his. "Have I told you recently that you're a very difficult woman?" he said finally.

Then unexpectedly he chuckled, a low sound that came from deep in his throat and crescendoed. His laughter, the relaxing of his grip on her arms broke the tension and Jennifer, feeling ridiculous standing there naked and arguing, laughed too.

"I give up," he said at last. "Just a kiss, Jennifer, one last one, since you're determined to leave me alone all night. It's not the way I want it to be, but I am trying to learn to be patient."

She smiled, knowing that patience didn't seem to be a virtue of his. "Then it will be a good lesson for you to learn," she said, a note of seriousness entering her humorous tone.

They faced each other, and somehow an understanding had come between them. She glanced past him to the beckoning bedroom beyond the window, wishing vaguely that everything were different.

"A kiss," he said quietly.

Seriously, she looked directly into his eyes he moved toward her. What did he feel? What did she? And where would this end? she asked herself. But then her lips were covered by his in a tender, loving caress. Was it possible that he really cared, that miracles came true?

"I'll walk you back."

"No. I'd rather be alone."

He didn't press the point but released her. "All right," he said. "If you're sure that's what you want."

She nodded.

"Good night," he said.

"Good night." She turned and walked away then, feeling self-conscious as she hurried along, grateful that the moon had gone behind clouds and aware of his eyes following her silvery form. And when she couldn't stand it any longer, she ran for the house.

# CHAPTER EIGHT

The following morning Jennifer wasn't surprised to hear a knock on the door, or when she opened it to find Flint, a tall brown grocery sack resting in the crook of one arm.

All morning she had tried to be sensible, practical about this. She was having an affair. All of her friends had had many. Why shouldn't she? There was no point in losing her head over it. But the eagerness in her voice when she said, "Come in," was apparent even to herself.

She turned then and walked ahead of him, aware of his eyes sweeping her hips snug in her jeans as he followed her. When she reached the kitchen, she faced the sink, looking fixedly out the window above it, unwilling to look into his eyes or reveal what might be in hers.

She heard him set down the groceries and come to stand behind her, and when she still didn't react, his fingers caressed the back of her neck as his arm circled her shoulders. Then his strength turned her to face him.

He seemed even taller. And his lips were compelling, hot, taking her into their own private world for a long melting moment before he raised his head and said, "Good morning."

It all seemed so natural, as if they did this every morning, and yet at the same time it seemed strange, completely foreign.

"Good morning," Jennifer returned.

He stepped back to the bag of groceries. "I brought

eggs, ham, English muffins, butter, lemons, and oranges to squeeze juice. What do you say to making eggs benedict?"

"Eggs benedict? But I told you I don't know how to cook!"

"Then I'll teach you. It's really just a matter of learning a few basics. You can help me."

His smile made his handsomely carved face seem almost boyish and she felt a warm surging in her insides that pulled her toward him, though her feet remained resolutely planted on the kitchen's tiled floor. It occurred to her that this was just how his other women must feel when they were with him. The thought took the edge off the magnetism drawing her toward him, so she was able to say, casually, "If you want to cook, it's up to you. I'll help, but don't say I didn't warn you."

He arranged all the ingredients and equipment on the counter first. Then, with a brief explanation about the cooking of eggs and the making of sauces, he showed her how to separate eggs, giving her a verbal recipe for hollandaise while he boiled water to coddle the eggs.

Toasting the muffins was easy, and she did that and squeezed the orange juice while he fried the ham; she was thankful that he made no comment when the frying pan he finally found was covered with dust. They worked together compatibly, and he didn't seem impatient when she broke an egg yolk on the ragged edge of shell.

Jennifer couldn't remember actually cooking with anyone since before her mother's accident. Then she had spent many an afternoon baking cookies and such. She remembered mixing huge bowls of batter and later licking them. It had been wonderful, a time when the world had been covered with a golden haze of contentment. How carefree everything had been then, she thought, sighing as she popped butter into the microwave to melt. And now she would leave all this so soon—that is, if she won the championship.

When everything was ready, they transferred it all to plates: the muffin, the ham, the coddled egg, and the hollandaise over it. Flint carried the plates to the table, putting hers before her as she was seated.

"This is delicious" she said, after she had taken a bite into her mouth. "Really wonderful, in fact."

"And what do you think? Was it that complicated?"

"No, you're right, maybe I won't be so hopeless as a cook after all."

"Everybody has to learn," he said. "And you're learning very well."

She glanced up at him, not sure any longer, by the hint of passion in his eyes, that he was talking about cooking. The expression vividly recalled the night before, and seeing him now so tall, so handsome, and somehow so utterly adorable in the bib apron he had found in a closet, it occurred to her that losing the championship didn't seem so terrible as it once had.

Her reverie jarred to a halt. Lose! She shook herself, taking hold of her thoughts. How could she even consider it? No, she would win, must win. She had planned to all her life, and anyway, it might be one thing to have an affair with this man, but it would never last, and she knew it. And if she lost it would mean being together for another month. Her thoughts were interrupted then by a knock on the front door.

"Oh, isn't this funny. You're Flint Michaels, aren't you? I remember seeing you at Jeff's party last night," said the shapely blond woman standing in the door. "We didn't get a chance to meet, but Jeff told me you didn't live far. And when my car broke down this morning in front of what must be your driveway, I was hoping someone would be home." She opened light-brown eyes in surprise. "I had no idea you lived here. And I'm so sorry to"—her breasts seemed suddenly more prominent—"to bother you. But maybe you could help me."

It seemed perfectly obvious to Jennifer that the woman was a phony, and it was annoying to see Flint falling for it.

"All right," he was saying, with a smile that drew a warm response from the woman. "Let's see your car."

"Out here," she said, turning to lead him.

They went together, disappearing down the driveway and slamming the door behind them. Jennifer picked up the dishes, unconscious of how hard she banged them as she loaded them into the sink.

Why should this affect her so? Her own relationship with Flint was just a physical thing, a fire that they couldn't avoid but that would burn itself out. Even Lillian had said no one would ever have Flint to herself, so why try to win a battle already lost? Forcing out of her mind the jealous images that threatened her, Jennifer rinsed the dishes, loaded them in the dishwasher, and headed for the barn, willing all her concentration to focus on the day's training. But King was in a rambunctious mood, as it turned out, rearing and bucking on the end of the lunge line so that Jennifer found herself pulled around the ring, fighting to control him. Then later he refused to stand still to be saddled, and he became even worse once she mounted him, bolting at any excuse, out of high-spirited energy, and refusing to obey.

His gaits and his timing were both terrible, and after a long session during which he seemed only to get worse, Jennifer decided that discretion was the better part of valor and brought him back to the barn.

She would have liked to blame their poor workout on King. But she knew, although she could barely admit it to herself, that King, being a sensitive horse, was undoubtedly only reacting, in large part, to her present tumultuous mood.

Damn Flint, she thought, rubbing King down with a sponge and a bucket of soapy water. It was really *his* fault.

145

She squeezed the sponge in her fist, and as the water dripped out in a thin stream she was unable to resist imagining that it was Flint's neck she was wringing. He was only using her. Why didn't that seem to make any difference? Last night had been one thing. But this morning he couldn't have been more eager to rush to the rescue of that woman who, she was absolutely sure, had purposely "broken down" in front of what she knew to be Flint Michaels' house. She was still sponging King's steaming body with vigorous strokes, when, moments later, she noticed Flint returning up the driveway, the blond woman nowhere in sight.

Jennifer turned her head in the opposite direction, pretending to be absorbed in her task as Flint strolled over to where King stood. Idly then, Flint picked the sponge out of the bucket and began running it over King again as if nothing could be amiss.

Out of the corner of her eye Jennifer watched, unwilling to let him have the satisfaction of seeing how upset she was managed to say, "Did you get the car fixed?" as if she were asking about the weather.

"Yes. It was nothing major. She had just run out of gas."

Jennifer kept her face turned away. *And if it wasn't anything major what took so long?* she wanted to ask, but she refrained. Still, he must have suspected her irritation, since he stopped sponging and looked at her over King's back.

"Can it be you're getting a little possessive, Jennifer? I thought that would be impossible for you."

Jennifer frowned and glanced at him, wondering if she had any secrets from this man. "I'm certainly not feeling possessive of you, if that's what you mean," she denied hotly.

"That is precisely what I mean. And," he continued, "I don't believe you."

146

"You don't have to believe it, I suppose," Jennifer stated flatly. "But I'm certainly not feeling possessive. On the contrary, I was just thinking how good it's going to be to *leave* you."

His expression remained unreadable as he stood looking at her, and it was probably because of this that she added," "You *did* realize I still planned on leaving?"

His gaze was considering, though he said nothing more before beginning to sponge down Desert King's long legs, bending at the waist to reach the horse's pasterns.

Jennifer continued holding the spraying hose on her side of the horse. His silence was even more irritating. But what had she expected, that he would ask her to stay? she thought, frustration concentrating in her chest and turning to a tight knot as she rinsed King's chest and neck.

She waited in vain for Flint to say something further. Evidently it was a closed subject for him. How easily he could dismiss her, she decided, pressing her thumb tighter over the hose spout and making the water squirt harder. And when he bent over further to rub the mud on the horse's back pasterns, and she was faced with the rear part of Flint's anatomy, she couldn't resist letting a corner of the spray reach him.

He stood up immediately and turned to look.

"Oh, I'm *so* sorry," she said, with obvious insincerity. "That was an accident. What a shame I got you wet."

She continued to wash down the horse, feeling him watching her for a moment longer before bending to his task again. And when he did, she couldn't help letting the water spout hit him again.

This time when he stood up the playful glint in his eye was dangerous, too. "You don't expect me to think *that* was an accident, do you?" he said. Then he was coming toward her, his back slightly hunched, his knees bent and ready to spring.

Jennifer knew she was no match for him, but seeing her

147

chance now, and heedless of the consequences, she pressed her thumb tight in the hose opening and squirted him directly in the face. He put up a hand to block the water, so it sprayed in every direction and back onto her as it hit his opened palm.

"Ahhk!" she cried, jumping two steps in the opposite direction—which was apparently just what he had in mind, since he followed, backing her toward a water trough. She pulled the hose away, dodging back before sending the spray to hit him full force from the side. Again he managed to block the water, forcing her back further though she managed to sidestep the trough as she continued to retreat onto the lawn.

There was no escape. He was fast, and never so big as now when he was closing in. "No!" she screamed, taking to her heels. But already he had her, wrestling the hose away and holding her fighting form as he squirted her full in the face.

She screamed against the cold, trying to raise her hands to cover her face. But he took both her hands in one of his and held them behind her. She pulled away, jerking as hard as she could, trying to throw him off balance, to trip him as he turned the hose on her breasts. Her boot made contact with his then, and suddenly they were both falling onto the grass and mud, still fighting, each with one hand on the hose that spouted haphazardly as they struggled for possession.

That Flint treated her with care made her feel ridiculously weak, so she fought harder. But when she did, Flint suddenly ended the battle by taking the hose. Just then, the water stopped, startling both of them.

Together they stared at the hose before following its green trail through the grass and across the mud to find King standing on it as he grazed unconcerned, effectively cutting off the water spray.

Still panting, they sat looking at each other. Both of

them were drenched and Flint's hair, dark with mud, was sticking to his face, the water dripping in rivulets over his forehead and down his nose and onto his shirt, which was equally muddy. Looking at him, Jennifer couldn't stop the laughter that burst out of her.

"What are you laughing at?" he asked, frowning, though his eyes twinkled as he indicated her with a waving gesture. "You haven't looked at yourself."

Jennifer looked down, not surprised to find her jeans and shirt equally smeared with mud—as was, undoubtedly, her face. Her laughter made her so weak she couldn't get up, and he was the first to stand, outstretching his hand.

She reached for it and he pulled her up, helping her brush the loose grass off her T-shirt. But the footing was slippery, and suddenly one red rubber boot had slipped to a particularly muddy section, sucking her sole down into the mush so that it didn't come out when she pulled.

She pulled harder, then jerked, feeling absurd. And when she did escape, with a mighty last try, it was only that her foot had come out of the boot, which remained as trapped as ever in the ooze. She lost her balance and fell down again.

This time it was Flint's turn to laugh, with cries of mirth from deep in his belly. Jennifer got up to stand on one foot, being unwilling to put her sock down in the mud.

She braced her hands on her hips. "You can stop now," she said, annoyed at being the subject of such wholehearted amusement. And when he didn't, she leaned forward to tackle him with such sudden, unexpected force that he was completely thrown off balance and landed abruptly in the mud, with her on top of him.

Still he was laughing, and Jennifer, taking advantage of the situation, grabbed one leg and removed a boot.

"Ha!" she said, throwing it over her shoulder to land not far from her boot.

His eyebrows were raised in surprise—at her audacity, she imagined. But it didn't stop him, just as she knew it wouldn't. And in a quick move he took her around her waist with one arm, freeing the other to quickly pull off her T-shirt and leave her standing in only her jeans and bra.

"Ha!" he said in return, throwing the T-shirt over his shoulder.

"Ohhh!" He really was insufferable, she thought, though she also knew her heart had begun to beat far too fast. How dare he! But then, looking from herself to him, she realized just how absurd this all was and began to laugh too, partly at themselves, partly to deny the barrier of intimacy that suddenly had been crossed. But he had stopped laughing, a flame of passion in his eyes as they ran over her. Then he took her hand and was leading her to the lawn. The hose had come back on again, so King apparently had moved. Without a word, Flint picked it up.

His touch held an intensity far different from that of a moment before, as he pulled her toward him and let the hose stream run over her shoulder, then higher to her cheek where his thumb brushed away caked mud. His eyes held hers as he let the water move along her shoulder and across her breasts.

Jennifer didn't trust her voice to speak. She continued to look at him, asking herself why it was impossible not to respond to him, to want his hands on her, stroking her as they were doing now. Yet a remaining fiber of sanity made her swallow hard and whisper, "Flint, not here, not now."

His hands continued moving over her, washing off the mud and grass with the hose, which no longer felt cold but, now that she was wet, would have seemed warm, even if his caressing fingers had not reawakened ready fires.

"Yes," he said, throwing the hose aside. "Here and

*now.*" He lifted her into his arms before sitting her on a part of the lawn still dry. Then he was pulling off her jeans and his own and lying beside her, kissing her, his arms circling round her back and holding her closer, pulling her deeper into his searching lips. His hands moved across the skin of her waist and belly. "Soft, soft," he whispered in her ear as the hands moved to her breasts.

She was trembling as he unsnapped the clasp of her bra, freeing them to his gaze, his touch, and finally his lips. She felt swept up in the irresistible current of passion and whirled beyond herself as his lips traveled from her breasts to her lips, then down her cheek to her throat pulse that raced like the hot Santa Ana winds.

He kissed her breasts again, more gently now, his lips coaxing her response as they moved lower to her navel, then he unzipped her jeans to go lower. He paused, but she didn't protest when he peeled off her pants and boots or when he knelt astride her prone body, pulling her to him.

When he entered her it was in one sure stroke that brought a cry of surprise and joy from the pit of her throat, and this time her own release came quickly, and then again, and even once more, until the world was a shower of lights, a fading, a whirling. Then it seemed she would lose consciousness as his pleasure erupted within her, adding a new, thrilling sensation.

They were both panting, swirling downward to finally lie side by side on the grass. Dimly the world came into focus when Jennifer found herself in the afternoon sun—Desert King grazing unconcerned several yards away and Flint still a part of her.

"This can't keep happening," she said finally, breathlessness still in her voice.

He laughed, tracing a finger around the outer circle of her breast, then swirling inward to touch that sensitive point that was still responding in spite of her will.

"What is between us can't be regulated like the water

coming out of that hose. What is between us has a life of its own and will continue to grow, whether you want it to or not."

Jennifer shook her head, although even then she knew it was true. As sanity returned, she did not stay with him but dressed, saying little before going to the house.

And later, lying alone in her bedroom, still quivering whenever she recalled the feel of his hands upon her, the smell of him, the hardness of him within her, she realized there was no way to fight it. Together they were like a natural force and what happened was as predictable and apparently uncontrollable as the law of gravity.

But there was no need to be swept away, she told herself. If men could have physical affairs with women, then why couldn't she have one with a man?

He had never mentioned love. No, love was not a part of this for either of them. Though, if he were different, she might love him—if she trusted him—but she didn't. A future with Flint was out of the question, and thinking about it would only invite unhappiness, she told herself. Why not just consider the present and enjoy the pleasure of the moment? It was such a short time until the championship, when she would leave the ranch permanently. Why not just let things go on . . .

And so for the next several days, as time brought the championship closer, Jennifer stopped fighting what her body had wanted all along and at night after cooking dinner together as had become their routine, she didn't avoid the arms that inevitably drew her close and made her once again melt into one pleasurable sensation after another. Soon, very soon—that is, if she won the championship—she would leave. Time enough then to consider it. So now as he spoke of the future she listened.

What did she think of planting their own alfalfa and irrigating the neglected orange orchards on the north side of the ranch? he asked. He was always interested to hear her opinions and ready to question or retort, so they spent every evening in conversations that made what used to be long nights speed past. He was so interesting to talk to, Jennifer thought, noticing that at least Flint never acted as though females were lesser than himself and therefore her ideas didn't matter. Instead he listened to her advice with interest, and as the days passed he put many of her suggestions into practice.

"I would have irrigated this orange grove years ago, if there'd been the money to do it," she told him one day as they walked through the trees that now were putting on new growth from the watering system Flint had installed. "Now there is the money," he said seriously. "And we'll get more than the investment in the watering system back in agricultural tax breaks."

Why hadn't her uncle known that, or indeed why hadn't she? thought Jennifer, impressed again with Flint's business wisdom. Yes, there were many attractive things about this capable man. But it wasn't until he had a party for the local "horse crowd," which was gathering in southern California for the National Championships, that she had to admit her relationship with Flint had changed everything. And yes, maybe she was even jealous as so many beautiful women fluttered around Flint and kissed and hugged him. But it wasn't until she overheard the conversation of a particularly lovely woman, quite young and well-dressed, that she realized the full extent of her own possessiveness.

"I've heard all about you," Regina Carson was saying. "Everyone thinks it's wonderful you've bought Casa Contenta and are going to join our little circle of Arabian horse owners," she continued, moving closer to Flint and watching him with half-closed, inviting eyes. "I bet you've made wonderful improvements already. Maybe later you could give me a tour."

Jennifer hardly noticed that Flint neither agreed nor

153

disagreed, deflecting Regina's question by asking one of his own. That wasn't the point. It was just that, seeing Regina with Flint, Jennifer suddenly realized that soon, after she left, Flint would quite possibly be sharing the ranch with another woman. This fact, which had been obvious from the first, suddenly hit her full force. The mistress of the ranch, *her* ranch, would be another woman.

But he doesn't love you, she reminded herself, watching Flint make a short remark that brought a gale of laughter from Regina and another woman who had joined them.

Yet, later in the evening when Flint danced with her, it did seem to Jennifer that there was a new gentleness in his touch, a certain warmth in the smile on his lips and a change in the lights in his eyes. Was she just imagining that his feelings for her were deepening? Could he come to care just for her? Or was he just using her, charming her into becoming his willing slave like so many others, a slave he would discard when the time came? And if he did care, wouldn't he ask her to stay on the ranch, win or lose?

It was a question that grew to dominate her thoughts. But then it seemed she had a way to test him when, several afternoons later, she received a letter from Leslie Barclay, a friend she had known in school who was now living in England. It was a long, chatty letter telling of the country life in England and then ending with questions about her, and an invitation.

You really must come to England this fall, Jennifer. We have great parties and fox hunts. (We don't actually kill the fox but drag the scent for the dogs to follow and the horses to chase after.) They are great fun really and we would all love you to come and stay as long as you like.

It would be a good opportunity, she thought, refolding

154

the letter and tapping it against her palm. She had decided to take an apartment in San Diego after the Nationals, but going as far away as London for a time might be a better, cleaner, break from here. But what would Flint think? Would he even care? And the next morning after breakfast, when Flint was thumbing through a stud book, Jennifer took the opportunity to read the letter aloud with a casual air.

She thought she would scream when a full minute passed in which he didn't react at all.

"Well, what do you think?" she asked finally, unable to stand his silence.

He continued looking intently into the book, and only shrugged. "Fox hunts are probably a lot of fun, and I know London is," he said emotionlessly. "You'd enjoy it." He paused, closed the book, and looked at the binding for a moment before turning to face her. "Is this the latest edition of the stud book?" he asked. "I don't see any of last year's foals listed in here."

"That's the one for last year," she said, impatiently walking to the shelf, grabbing the book, and slamming it into his hand. "If you read carefully you would see it's the wrong one," she finished coldly, starting to walk away.

"Hey, wait a minute," he said, putting down the book and walking across the room to block her path out the door. "What's the matter with you?"

"I'm not sure I want to talk about it now, Flint. I thought you might have an opinion about my going to England. That's all."

"I do have an opinion," he said, frowning. "But I want you to do what you want to. Anyway, as I recall, my opinions never meant much to you."

Jennifer stared at him. "You're right," she said at last, coolly lifting her chin. "It's not important what you think."

She turned away then, jerking her arm free and walking

out the door. He had said all he needed to, and her emotions suddenly felt covered with a sheet of ice, a feeling that wouldn't let her speak further or even look at him again that afternoon, as they packed the saddles and bridles and loaded the truck before leading Desert King into the trailer and heading south.

It was almost four hours and two hundred miles north of San Diego along the coast to Del Mar, a village town where both racing and horse showing were regular events.

The Del Mar track and fairgrounds were a complex of white fences and barns, a ring with covered grandstands for horse showing, and a track and larger stands for racing. "Where the Turf Meets the Surf" was the motto in large red letters stretched on a banner across the main street. But Jennifer hardly noticed, and when they pulled into the show grounds she hopped out of the truck to get stall and room assignments from the show office.

"Barn B 4," Jennifer said when she reentered the truck. It was the first thing either of them had said in hours. They were quick to unload King and get him settled in a stall thick with hay in one of the old adobe brick barns. Their rooms were over the barns, and Jennifer was surprised to find Flint had ordered two separate rooms.

"Two rooms?" she asked, before she could stop herslf from seeming surprised.

"It doesn't matter," was all he said, putting her things in one of the rooms and his in the other.

She was glad when he didn't follow her downstairs. She didn't want him to see her face—the disappointment she knew was there. So she didn't stay around the barns after checking King but went to dinner alone, satisfying her hunger with the fare from one of the small food stands on the grounds and chatting with several of the other competitors milling around until long after it was dark. Then, returning to her room, she climbed the stairs and was just inserting the key in the lock when she heard Flint's voice.

"What are you doing?" he asked, as if she were entering a room that was not her own.

He was on the stair landing looking at her. "I'm going to my room," she whispered, aware it was late and not wanting to wake anyone already sleeping in the adjoining rooms.

He came closer. She couldn't make out his features in the dark but could feel his breath on her cheek as he said, "You didn't think you were actually going to sleep in there?"

"But you said it didn't matter," she challenged. "I thought . . ."

His laugh interrupted her as he came closer, leaning to scoop her up, so suddenly she was in his arms, being carried down the hall to his room. "Did you really think we were going to sleep separately?" He laughed again. Then the key was in the lock, the door was swinging open, and he was kicking it closed behind him.

# CHAPTER NINE

When the door closed Jennifer began to struggle but he paid no attention, his face serious, intense, as he pulled her closer, higher in his arms and buried his head between her breasts, kissing her, pulling her western shirt with his teeth so it unsnapped in a series of pops, leaving only her sheer peach bra between them.

"Jennifer," the word came from deep within him, an urgent cry. And from her innermost self Jennifer felt an answering need that merged her body with his as his kiss tasted, savored, explored her lips, her mouth, and a rush of warm tingling delight fired her own desires.

Yet she resisted them. Things couldn't go on this way. They had to talk. And so she said, "Making love is not going to solve anything."

"Maybe not," he said, walking to the bed and tossing her on it with a bounce before sitting down to remove his shoes. "But it's not a bad way to begin."

His confidence in her acquiescence couldn't have been more casual if they had been married twenty years. He stood and unbelted his jeans, slipping them down his slim hips, stepping out of them.

He bent close as he laid them at the foot of the bed. But now there was a question in his expression as he leaned to kiss her again.

She pushed him away, getting up to face him, her hair tousled, her lips still red from his kisses. He started coming closer, but she thrust out a hand. "No, Flint. Please. I want to talk."

He stopped, having learned to read the firmness of her mood by the position of her chin, noticing that the slant was more pronounced than ever. He sat on the bed, a hand on one raised knee as he cocked his head and said, "Okay, Jennifer. What is it?"

Jennifer hadn't rehearsed her words and now, confronted with his attention, she wasn't sure for a moment how to begin, but then she said, "I don't belong to you, that's all. I've told you before, you've bought the ranch but you haven't bought me. You don't have any right to do what you just did. The people that are here showing horses I've known for most of my life. So even if it was all right between us for you to carry me like that down the hall, which it isn't, I wouldn't want you to do that here and now when any of them could have seen me."

"Okay." His voice was understanding. "I didn't think of that." His gaze moved over her. "I was thinking how beautiful you are with your hair like that." He held out his arms, a warm half-circle that beckoned. "Come here."

In her deepest heart, Jennifer longed to go to him, and it took all her self-control to keep her back rigid, her hands clenched against the feeling of weakness that threatened to overwhelm her. "And I want to tell you that this has got to stop happening," she said. "It can't continue like this. We've been having an affair, that's all. But that doesn't mean it's a permanent arrangement, and I don't want you to start acting like it is."

"And what is 'it' for you?" he asked, his voice containing a measured evenness. "What do you want?"

"Something far less intimate, as I've tried to tell you. I'm not a fool. I realize what brought us together. You wanted this ranch and you've managed to buy it and force me to work for you."

"Yes, that's how we got here. Is that all there is to it for you?"

She looked away from him. "It's true I find you attractive."

"That's some concession," he said, crossing his arms. His eyes narrowed. "Look, Jennifer, why don't you say what you're trying to say? You think that I've forced you into everything that's happened, and now you're calling a halt."

"I don't think you've forced me, but I am calling a halt. I don't belong to you. I'm not some kind of toy, Flint, and I want you to stop treating me like one!"

"I don't think of you as a toy."

"You do! I want something lasting, Flint, not something that gets thrown away when the novelty is gone. I want the biggest part of a man's heart, not just the time he has for recreation."

There, she thought, she'd said it. Now if he would just tell her she was wrong—that he did care for her—that she did have the biggest piece of his heart. But he only looked at her.

"Okay Jennifer," he said, after a long time. "If that's what you see in what has been between us, I guess that's what it is for you."

She came toward him, snatching her shirt from under his knee and angrily putting it on. "I'm my own woman, Flint Michaels, so I'm going to sleep in my own room tonight and until after the championship and my obligation to you is over!"

She opened the door, half expecting at any moment to feel his large hand encircle her upper arm and hold her back. Her wildest hopes even speculated that he might tell her that their relationship meant far more to him than she suspected. But none of that happened. Instead she was allowed to walk to her door and slam it behind her with a resounding bang that challenged him—dared him to try to stop her.

When she reached her own room she threw herself full-length on her bed, the blanket rubbing roughly against her cheek as she waited. He wouldn't leave things like this. He would come and declare himself one way or another. He would at least ask her to stay on at the ranch even if she did win. But as she listened with growing alertness to every sound she could discern through the thin walls, she heard only the creak of the closet door, wooden hangers scrapping along the pole, his footsteps, then nothing more, so she soon realized he was already in bed.

She flipped over then, lying on her back, her arms crossed, her lips compressed tightly. All this only proved one thing. Everything she thought about him was true. If he wanted her, he would want to straighten things out. But he didn't, and the logical side of her character was surprised that, instead of feeling satisfied that at last she knew the truth for sure, she felt stabbing betrayal. A single tear swelled out of her eye and trembled down her cheek before she brushed it away. He would never change—she would be a fool to wait for the final humiliation. She wouldn't tell him what she planned. She wouldn't even speak to him unless she had to. Then immediately after the championship she would get on that plane for London and leave all this behind.

She didn't know how long she slept, fitfully tossing and turning, refusing to think of Flint and yet unable to put him out of her mind. And she thought she was still dreaming when suddenly he was above her, his dark furred chest revealed in the soft glow of the flashlight he set on the floor.

The belligerence was gone from his face. His eyes caressed her. His long fingers were tracing the line of her jaw, her throat, then lower, with such gentleness even while they renewed that now familiar fire. And suddenly,

161

with the clouds of sleep insulating her from all logic or worldly consideration, Jennifer knew with sudden overwhelming certainty that she loved him.

"Jennifer, Jennifer, I want you to trust me," he whispered, a catch in his words that went directly to a deep-felt nerve.

She could not speak at once, a tightness closing her throat and making swallowing necessary and difficult. So instead, impulsively, she reached out her arms and parted them as her ragged voice called "Flint!"

He was kissing her then, his chapped lips slightly rough against hers as her took full possession of her mouth for a timeless moment before drawing away. Frustration, concern, seduction all combined in his expression as he remained bent over her, his gaze searching her face. And when he seemed to find what he sought, his mouth came down again, this time demanding her response.

Now her lips parted easily. And when they did he was gentle again, seeming to want all of her in his mouth, to taste her, to feel the shape of her lips, the corners of her mouth as his hands held her face, his fingers working into her hair and brushing it back from her temples. She felt engulfed not only by his size but by the intensity of her own response as his touch opened a tingling in her abdomen, a wanting, a building within her, encircling her, surrounding her as sure as his arms that pulled her closer.

She didn't fight the melting sensation that overcame her—that sent her mind beyond anything but this big man above her. His hands took her breasts now, cupping their outer size, weighing them in his palm as he reached beneath the long cotton nightgown where her flesh was naked and vulnerable, his thumbs touching her nipples as his kisses were passing down her throat.

Part of the covers were still on her, and he tossed them aside before reaching to pull the nightgown over her head.

162

She sat up, the points of her exposed breasts nearly brushing his chest, jiggling as she lifted her arms, letting the cotton material be drawn over her head, sliding soft along her arms before it was tossed on the floor.

He slipped off his unbelted jeans, the only thing he had worn. And then he was pushing her down on the bed. His weight settled over her as he opened her knees and came between them. Then he was kissing her cheeks, her mouth, her eyes, before moving to the hollow behind her ear, sending thrilling sensations chasing over her flesh, each movement issuing a new tremor, like ocean waves building one on the other.

He moved lower. Her navel became an object of curiosity that his tongue explored in tiny caresses, wanting to know every crevice both large and small as he traveled even lower.

Jennifer gasped as the fire burned with hot licking flames, taking her to unknown pleasures until she thought she would burst and colors washed across her inner vision. Then, just before she could bear it no more, his body was moving higher, his weight resting on his forearms, his hands touching her face, cradling her head, as slowly, so she felt every bit of him, the barrier between them was no more. Her head whirled and she felt herself panting for breath as his movements began slowly, so she was aware of all of him, then increased in momentum, taking her passion to a higher, giddier plane.

If only he would stop—if only he would never stop. And as the entire world focused itself so it was only them, an inner voice whispered, *I love him, I love him,* as at last the wave crested and she was cascading over the top, then swirling down, down, unaware that she moaned his name into his mouth before once again she lay quiet in his arms.

That was not the last time they made love.

All through the night their passions rekindled, drawing them together with the irresistible strength of magnets, driving them to spend themselves before falling asleep again until, all too soon, the night became day.

When Jennifer awoke the next morning, it was within the embrace of his arms and filled with a satiation she had never known. And from that moment and for the next three days, she put the future out of her mind, concentrating instead on the present and their time together.

They spent the days working Desert King, Flint watching her as she rode over jump after jump, her form reflecting the approving admiration in his eyes.

At sunset they rode together down to the beach, stopping the horses at the edge of the surf and letting them paw and splash as they watched the sky turn to lavender and then vermilion. And the nights they spent again as lovers.

Occasionally she told herself this couldn't go on, and she asked herself if she could bear to lose twice in love. But this small voice was overpowered by another, stronger, need that wanted to believe he might be falling in love with her too. If only he would, oh, how she longed to admit her own newly discovered feelings, to say, "I love you," and have him take her in his arms and cover her face with kisses and tell her he wanted her to stay with him forever. But even as the days wore on, secret moments out of time, a fairy tale before the eventual, inescapable reality, a shred of caution kept her from admitting what she felt, of becoming another openly worshipful female like the dozens that already swarmed around him, whose adulation seemed to bore him. No, if she told him how she felt and he rejected her she couldn't stand it. And she could almost imagine the look of surprise touched with triumph and even pity that would come to his face. She needed more time, and more and more she recalled their bargain. "If you win the championship in November you can consider the contract fulfilled a month early," he had told her.

"And what if I lose?"

"Then you'll have to stay the extra time, Jennifer. I

have to give you some incentive. And getting away from me seems to be the strongest one available."

Oh, how things had changed from that time. How could she ever have known that being with him would become so important? It wasn't fair, and yet there was no choice for it. And more and more she realized she must somehow lose.

It was a foreign, horrible alternative at first, and lying in bed with him, his arms possessively around her, she knew she had wanted the championship more than anything all her life. And she knew Flint wanted it too. But what did a trophy and blue ribbon really mean if it meant they would be parted? She was a woman in love, and what kind of a woman was she if she didn't do everything she could to try to make him love her back?

It was the hardest choice she had ever made. But as the day of the first eliminations came, she made up her mind to lose.

It began as an overcast day, typical for the seaside of Del Mar. But then, like magic, the haze disappeared and the sky became an intense blue.

They would jump in three rounds, and the ten best times and scores would determine the ten finalists. How easy it was going to be just to pull up on the last jump, to eliminate herself, she thought as she entered the ring. But she quickly discovered that the hours and days and years of training Desert King made him jump with eager pride, in spite of her subtle attempts to slow him down. And as she exited the second round still without faults, a strange feeling was rolling her insides.

It would be just as easy to pull him up in the finals, and accepting Flint's thumbs-up sign with a smile, Jennifer went in for the third round and went clean.

"You're unbeatable," Flint told her later, after an intimate dinner *à deux* during which they celebrated her inclusion into the finalists.

"Overconfidence is dangerous," she said. "There were several other times as good as mine, and Jeff Adams' horse had an even better one."

"But you won't let him beat you," Flint said. "You've wanted this too badly to let anything stand between you and this championship."

He toasted her then and she smiled, careful to hide the war within herself which his words underlined and which she felt more pointedly with each hour as they ticked off to the inescapable final moment when she would enter the ring.

He guided her to her own room that night, unlocking the door but making no move to step inside.

"Tonight you rest," he said. "Tomorrow you'll need all your strength."

In keeping with her own casualness about their relationship, she nodded, not wanting him to realize how necessary their lovemaking had become. "Good night," he said, leaning down to kiss her.

Their lips met, and though it seemed he too wanted the kiss to be matter-of-fact, she couldn't help that her lips parted, inviting his tongue, which gently caressed hers as she leaned into the hand that caressed her breast. The kiss went deeper, longer, and she could feel his hard need of her through their clothes before they finally parted.

"You're heady as wine," he rasped huskily, holding her away from him. "I'm beginning to think rest isn't so important, after all."

His eyes were soft and full of a light that seemed to border on a new depth of feeling. Then he stood even straighter, pushing her more firmly now into her room. "Sleep well," he said, taking her fingers and kissing them.

"I will, and good night," she said, wishing she could find a way to prolong the moment, wanting to tell him her feelings, to admit everything and count on that new emotion she had seen in his face and felt in his voice. And yet, stepping inside, she closed the door.

It was a horrible night in which she learned more fully than ever how necessary their nights together had become. And she tossed and turned, unable to sleep, only to rise well before dawn.

She knew Flint, though an early riser, wouldn't be up for hours. Feeling a fluttering nervousness in her stomach, along with a need to be alone to fight the battle raging within her, she dressed and went downstairs to the barns.

By the time Flint arrived, obviously puzzled by her disappearance, she was already having Desert King saddled.

"What happened to you this morning? I thought we were going to have breakfast together."

"I couldn't sleep," she said shortly, "and I'm not hungry."

She kept her face turned away as he spoke. "It's a big day today. Anyone would be nervous. Is there anything I can do?"

"No," she said, her voice barely above a whisper. "I think you've done enough."

She knew she was behaving strangely, but again the strength of her emotions seemed to demand it. Wanting to separate herself from him completely, she turned her attention away, trying to concentrate all of it on King as she mounted and adjusted the reins in her hand.

*Flint, oh, Flint,* a voice inside her cried out as she rode away. Oh, God, but she couldn't think about him now. So forcing him out of her mind, Jennifer kept her eyes fixed directly ahead as she trotted King toward the ring.

The steward was there, his derby off and the inside filled with papers, each with a number on it.

Pulling King to a halt, Jennifer dismounted to stand among the others, then reached into the hat to pull out one of the papers. Number nineteen. She would be last. A good

167

position in that she would know the time she had to beat, a bad one since the track between the jumps, presently graded smooth, would be roughened and therefore more dangerous to ride at high speed.

She called out her number and the steward wrote down the order of contestants, wishing each of them luck before disappearing into the ring through the big gates.

Over the loudspeakers, the judges were being introduced, and applause followed the introductions. Then the national anthem was being played.

She rode King slowly around the make-up arena as the first horse took the course, trying to keep her nerves and King's calm and collected.

King was in excellent form, at the apex of conditioning, the height of perfection, and something inside Jennifer swelled large with pride, knowing he was the best. Several fellow competitors passed by, wishing her luck, and she returned their wishes in kind. The air was growing more intense, touching a basic part of her. It was a day she had dreamed of for so long and yet there was Flint. If only she hadn't fallen in love.

Then Jeff Adams approached, a cold glint in his eyes as he assessed first Desert King, then Jennifer. In equal measure Jennifer watched him. Indeed, his stallion Argos looked in excellent condition, prancing with energy yet under control. Jeff wheeled the stallion close to King, and she felt her horse stiffen as the stallion rolled his eyes and would have struck with a forefoot had Jeff not checked him.

Jeff laughed. "Argos is spoiling for a fight," he commented. "How is King doing?"

"He's working fine," Jennifer said shortly, wanting to get rid of Jeff so she could continue to focus her attention on the coming competition. Jeff leaned closer.

"Listen, Jennifer. Remember what I told you at the party the other night. I meant it then and I mean it now."

168

He smiled slyly. "I don't know what allegiance you owe Flint after he bought the ranch out from under you, anyway. I'd say you don't owe him a thing. My offer of a job is still open. But to sweeten the deal—well, if for some reason King should lose today, it means ten grand for you."

In Jeff's face was a look that recalled their old acquaintance and urged her to do the same. But she only stared at him. It sickened her that he had actually offered her a bribe, and a fury rumbled in her chest at the insult; though not wanting to spoil her concentration by losing her temper, she said, "I agree with you Jeff. I don't owe Flint anything. But I'm not winning for him, I'm winning for me. I've always wanted this, trained for it. And now I'm going to do my best to win. Money isn't an issue and neither—neither is anything else."

As she spoke, Jennifer suddenly knew it was true. Yes, even while she did love Flint, foolishly, hopelessly, nothing could make her purposely lose this championship. She had been even more ridiculous to think she could. This was in her blood, this thrill of horses and competition, and no one, not even Flint, could make her stop short of accomplishing her dreams.

"All right, Jennifer. Have it your own way. I don't think King can beat Argos. I just thought, for old time's sake, that I could be generous with an old friend, and I know you must need the money."

"The best horse will win. And I assume that, since you're willing to bribe me, you must agree with me that the best horse is King and not Argos. Now, if you'll excuse me."

She turned King away just as Argos struck out with a front foot again, his iron-shod hoof barely missing King and Jeff doing nothing to prevent it. Gritting her teeth and narrowing her eyes, she stared at Jeff, who only smiled with a superior air as she continued to ride away.

King was trembling with anger as she guided him out of sight of Argos beyond several practice jumps. "Easy, easy boy," she said, stroking his neck, which had tensed at the challenge of the other stallion, watching the muscles on it rippling as she controlled her fury.

Jeff had done that purposely, but there was nothing to do about it. Such competitions were often determined by the war of nerves in the make-up ring, and she wasn't going to lose hers.

She walked King around slowly, waiting for her number to be called and realizing from the cheers of the crowd that the other horses must be doing well. And after she heard the announcer score six clean performances, she realized first place would be determined by which horse was able to complete the course in the shortest time without touching or knocking down any fences.

Jeff's number was called next. Turning his horse in a neat spin toward the gate, he urged Argos into a long trot and swept beyond the gates.

Argos' pure whiteness always made the crowd catch its breath as he entered, and Jennifer heard the unified gasp as he circled and then took the course. She wanted to ignore his performance and simply hear the results but, drawn by curiosity, she urged King to the side gate, where she could look over and watch as the big stallion glided around the course, taking the jumps effortlessly, as if he had wings, and at a speed just approaching danger.

Her practiced eye could detect a slippery spot from the skidding marks at the far end of the ring, and as Jeff neared the spot she saw his horse slow, take the jump before it, and land squarely; his two front feet skated momentarily, then recovered before going on to clear the next three jumps and cross the finish line.

The stopwatches were pushed and consulted before the time was announced. Fifty-one seconds flat.

Jennifer's heart pounded wildly. Argos' time equaled

her best performance. If she was to win, then Desert King would have to go faster than he had ever gone, slick spot or no slick spot.

They called her number then, and steeling herself, she leaned forward, patting King again as she remembered Flint's words. "You'll win. You want this too badly to let anything stand between you and the championship."

Her number was called again, bringing her thoughts sharply to the present and, adjusting her hat, she trotted toward where the ringmaster held the gate open.

Desert King knew the time had come as he pulled at the bit impatiently. They made a small circle just inside the gate before she guided him onto the course. She heard the click of the stopwatch as she passed the starting line and urged Desert King on to the first jump.

As they approached the first jump his black ears, small and sculptured, stood erect, pointing directly toward it, and he took it eagerly, in a single bound, clearing it easily. He seemed to know what was expected of him, and it was unnecessary for Jennifer to urge him on; rather she had to pull him up slightly as the next in a series of speeding leaps brought him to the end of the ring at such speed that it seemed impossible to make the turn without a spill. But King scrambled around the turn without slowing down, then headed for the next series of jumps, moving faster and faster, his head high, his eyes eager, his nostril snorting in air as if he knew how important this round of jumps was. And seeing the big horse's excitement and intense spirit, Jennifer, wondering how she could have ever considered losing, leaned low over King's neck and let the big horse have his head.

As they raced across the finish line she felt the applause and cheers ringing in her ears, and when the spectators gave her a standing ovation she stopped to salute the crowd before trotting briskly out the ring exit. All of them could see, even before they heard her time, that hers would be the best.

Already a crowd was gathering around her outside the ring, and with a mixture of pride and a terrible sinking in the pit of her stomach, Jennifer faced Flint as he came out of the stands toward her, his hand being shaken by well-wishers many times before he reached her.

"You were magnificent," he told her, with genuine admiration in his eyes. The constriction in her throat at the sight of his handsome features, at the touch of his hand, wouldn't let her say more than "Thank you," before she reached down to pat King so that her face would be turned away.

Again the applause was thunderous as her time of 50.7 seconds was announced and Jennifer rode King back into the ring, the new champion.

It seemed suddenly as if she might actually be dreaming it all as she cantered Desert King into the center of the ring, where photographers' lights flashed in showers of bright light as she proudly turned King to squarely face the judge's box. A collar of roses was pinned around his neck and a silver tray was held up to her. More camera flashes went off as she smiled.

No, none of it seemed real, even with several members of the press waiting for her outside the ring. "Dallas Forman, *Arabian Horseman* magazine . . . How does it feel to win the championship at last, Miss Globe?" one asked, pencil poised.

Jennifer answered all their questions briefly and automatically, keeping her eyes turned toward the crowd surrounding Flint. She was only thumped down to reality when a woman from the *San Diego Final Union* asked, "And what are you going to do now? I understand the ranch has been sold."

She turned to the reporter, and when she realized she had been staring silent for too long, trying to decide just what she was going to do, she said suddenly, "I'm going to leave the country."

It was as if life coursed back into her as she turned the horse toward the barn. Her chin came up and she felt herself looking life square in the eye. What else was there to do? She had won, not lost, and she couldn't stay on the ranch without acknowledging her feelings to Flint and taking the chance of his rejection. She would have to go. Obviously he didn't want her, or he would already have asked her to stay. Better to go now rather than having to face the fact that he didn't love her, and wouldn't it be better this way?

Approaching the crowd, she noticed Flint in the center of a group of women laughing and talking animatedly as champagne corks flew in the air. Then, as they saw her, they all turned and applauded until they were facing her with broad smiles of congratulation.

Flint raised his glass. "To Jennifer, the best damn rider —" she heard him begin, but the rest of the toast was lost to her, the light in his face touching every nerve deep within, so again she was aware of the acute, agonizing depth of love she felt for this man.

It was a moment of great triumph, a day she had rehearsed a million times, and yet now everything was different, starkly, horribly different. Even this rising in her heart passed quickly and she was left again with a vast hollowness roaming her stomach.

*You could have lost,* a small voice admonished. Then she pushed the thought aside. She loved him, yes, but a woman shouldn't have to give up everything for any man; he should have met her part of the way.

She dismounted, slipping slowly to the ground. How odd it was that no one noticed her soberness in the midst of their own eagerness for celebration. They must imagine her in shock—well, she was.

173

Taking King's bridle, she led him through the crowd—Patty and Grant Williams, the Becks, the DuPonts, a brace of stable boys eager to add their praise. Congratulations, congratulations. She was kissed and hugged wherever she turned, and no one seemed to guess that the occasional tear rolling down her cheek was not from happiness.

# CHAPTER TEN

Jennifer moved steadily through the crowd. "Thank you. Yes. How kind. Yes, thank you."

They were people she had known for years, and yet suddenly none of their words of praise could fill the cavern within her. Even *this* was Flint's triumph. Now he had the ranch, the championship, and even the adoration of these people, she thought, reaching the edge of the crowd and breaking away to lead King to his stall.

Across the barn aisle Argos was being sponged down and stalled by one of Jeff's grooms. The stallion seemed in a nasty temper, pawing and stamping just as if he knew he had lost. He bellowed defiantly, tossing his pure white head so his mane danced like silvery flames about his heavily muscled neck.

Reacting to the stallion's challenge, Desert King tried to pull away, prancing with excitement, so Jennifer took a firmer hand on his rope to guide him into his stall.

"Congratulations, Miss Globe. "You're the best lady rider I've ever seen."

She nodded her acknowledgment, smiling wanly, trying to unsnap the lead rope from King's halter and unable to as he pranced in place, his long neck stretched over his stall door, his chest pressed hard against it as he called out again.

"Easy, easy, King," she said, putting a hand on his churning shoulder.

Argos' fierce call rang out again, and this time crashing sounds followed as Argos' hooves hit his own door. The noise continued, enraging King further until, with a mighty leap, he hit the wooden barrier, popping it open and plunging out in a bound that accelerated into a gallop as he dashed toward Argos' stall.

Jennifer tried to hold the rope, but it was pulled through her hands, burning them before it jerked free and trailed behind King. Hearing King coming, Argos bellowed a louder, more frenzied challenge and kicking his front legs, smashed his own door, bolting through the splintered opening.

In the open the stallions faced each other, one stark white, the other glittering black. And later Jennifer would recall only flashes of memory made more intense by the terror that marked those moments as the two stallions rose on their hind legs and struck out in a thrashing of hooves and slashing of teeth.

Blood was drawn on both horses even before Jennifer could leap after King to catch the end of his halter rope, pulling with all the strength of her shoulders and arms, jerking, leaning all her weight against the rope. But the might of the enraged stallion was such that, with a swing of his neck, she was taken into the air and pulled between the warring giants.

"King," she screamed. But her voice was drowned out by the crash of bodies overhead.

She tried to get to her feet, but found herself knocked down and scrambling again. There was a horrible pain against her leg, then a strange numbness; the cries of stallions accompanied those of men as everyone nearby gathered around to separate the warring animals. She heard Flint's voice above the others.

A hoof stamped, just missing her ear. Then she was being pulled up and away by the back of her shirt and coat, half dragged, half carried as she heard muffled cursing.

176

She had already wrapped her arms protectively around her head, and now, pulling down the shield, she saw Flint —question, relief, fury all crossing his pale face. And there was Jeff too, suddenly reaching down to help her up, though Flint moved in his way.

"I can take care of Jennifer," he said. "For the time being, at least, she is still my responsibility."

The two men stood facing each other, circled by grooms and owners who glanced from them to one another. But no one said anything and Jeff didn't move to stop Flint as he picked her up and carried her to a bench in the stall they had converted to a tack room.

"Damn it, Jennifer! What a stupid thing to do! Are you all right?"

He loomed over her, his features taut and stricken. "Yes," she nodded. "Yes I'm all right. It's just . . ."

"Just what? Where are you hurt?"

"I'm all right, I said." She raised herself up and glared at him. "And stop yelling at me. Someone had to separate them, and it didn't look like you were doing anything but celebrating."

"Well, I certainly wouldn't have jumped into the middle of a stallion fight. What's gotten into you, trying to separate them by yourself!"

"I told you not to yell at me!" She stood up, feeling light-headed and swaying slightly, though she covered it by grabbing a nearby saddle rack for support. "Just leave me alone, Flint. You've already done enough without making things worse."

Her pants leg was torn up to her groin and she felt absurd standing there, although the crowd now seemed more occupied with separating the two horses and checking them for injuries.

Jennifer wanted to rush forward and see if King was hurt but an overwheiming dizziness kept her standing by the hay for fear of fainting as Flint went to see himself.

"Take him over here," he ordered a groom. "He's not going to calm down until he can't see Argos."

The stallions were hauled in opposite directions, two men on each animal. Then, as King stopped dancing and pulling against his lines, Jennifer watched Flint kneel and check the stallion's legs. She could tell by his face that there were no serious injuries, and she breathed an inward sigh of relief.

Now, if only she could feel better. If only she could just leave now before he could stop her. This morning she had packed her things in a small suitcase and put it in the tackroom. And getting up now, she took it in hand and headed back toward the main ring, where she knew taxis would be waiting.

As she went on everything seemed hazy, distant, slightly unreal, but she forced her mind to focus on a single need. She had to leave now, before she would have to face the humiliation of his not wanting her.

If only her leg didn't hurt. As she walked one boot squished as if it were filled with water.

She must go—must go.

She didn't expect the hand that so uncompromisingly took her elbow. And she nearly fell, except that suddenly she was against the barn's side.

"And where do you think—"

He stopped in mid-sentence, his face changing from brazen confrontation to sudden concern.

Jennifer watched him, unaware of her own whiteness, or how she swayed, only aware that she was caught, caught. And with the instinct of a cornered animal, she fought back. "Let me loose, Flint," she said, her voice sounding odd and far away, even to herself.

He was looking at her torn pants and, following his eyes, she noticed one side was sticking wetly to her leg. Reaching down, she touched it, staring at the fingers that came away red.

"Let me see that leg, Jennifer."

"No!" she said automatically, seeing all her hopes for escaping vanish. "No! No! No!"

But resistance was out of the question when he picked her up and carried her a few steps to an open stall filled high with fresh straw, where he laid her down.

She tried to struggle, but his strength gave no quarter; taking opposite sides of the material in his two hands, he ripped the pants leg open to reveal a gash in her leg and a pulsing rivulet of blood dripping into her boot.

Vaguely she puzzled over the lack of pain before absently recalling that large wounds often remained numb for an extended period. But this thought was overridden by Flint as he cursed quietly and called someone over his shoulder.

"Flint." She tried to stand.

"Jennifer, for once in your life shut up and let something be done for you before you bleed to death." But already his face, the barn, the sounds beyond the stall seemed distant, hazy, then darker, darker, as it seemed she was falling, falling. Vaguely she thought, *I'm going to die, and now he will never know I love him,* before everything disappeared.

"Jennifer, Jennifer." The voice was somewhere over her head, calling her, expecting her to answer. Yet clouds, mist, separated them.

She tried to lift her eyelids, heard someone moan, then realized that it was her own voice.

There was a dark shape over her that slowly focused into a face. Yes, Flint, his eyes full of concern even as he smiled and called her name with a note in it which sent a certain answering vibration into her body.

"Flint," she whispered, lolling her head from side to side. "What? . . . how? . . ." Her eyes circled the room. White. Everything was white, the bed, the curtains, even the telephone and the stand where it rested. "I thought I'd died," she said, recalling how she had dropped into the darkening tunnel in what seemed only the moment before.

He laughed, and there was a twinkle in his eyes. "No, you're not dead. In fact, the doctors assure me that as soon as that leg heals you'll be good as new, although you did give us all something to worry about for a while."

"But how? What happened?"

"You fainted, that's all. You'd lost a lot of blood. But now you're going to be fine."

Jennifer moved her arms, her legs, aware then of the bandage on her thigh. "It was bad?" she asked.

"Very bad," Flint replied, recalling the high-speed trip to the hospital, and a depth of fear he had never known.

"Well, so I see you're awake."

Both Jennifer and Flint turned to see a tall gray-haired man standing in the doorway, a doctor by his clothes, who came into the room and peered down at her.

Flint introduced them. "This is Dr. Saben."

The doctor smiled down at her. "You've given Mr. Michaels here quite a scare. He hasn't left this room for twenty-four hours." He smiled more broadly. "And I'm particularly glad to see you're recovered. I certainly didn't want to be the one who had to pry him away from you if your stay turned out to be extended."

Still smiling, Dr. Saben came closer and bending, listened to her heart and took her pulse. "You're fine now," he pronounced, "at least fine enough to leave here, though you'll have to stay in bed for at least a week."

"When, when can I go h—" She glanced at Flint, remembering suddenly that the ranch was no longer her home. "When can I leave the hospital?"

"By tomorrow morning, I think, if everything remains normal. But you will have to promise only bed rest until that leg is well on its way to healing." He turned to Flint. "You'll see she's taken care of?"

Flint nodded, and Jennifer noticed the firm look in his eyes.

"Nice meeting you, Jennifer," the doctor was saying before nodding to Flint. "And you too, Mr. Michaels." Then he was gone.

Jennifer remained silent as the doctor's words sank in, bringing her dilemma into focus again. Well, Flint could think that he was going to keep her under his control, but he wasn't. And something within her that for a moment had been vulnerable was now forced to harden. She turned away from him, refusing to look at the face that had become so beloved.

"I want to leave here, Flint," she said at last in a low serious voice.

"Good! I'll take you tomorrow." He walked to the closet. "Your clothes are here." He held up the torn, blood-stained breeches. "The blouse is okay, but these are hardly wearable. I bought you some jeans to wear home," he said, seeming completely offhand, as if nothing had changed.

"Flint . . . I'm not going to the ranch. I've decided to leave."

He looked at her as if she had just said something more than slightly ridiculous. "And where were you planning on going? You can't get out of bed for a week."

"I'm not sure. I'll have to make arrangements. I have friends I can stay with, and Richard has an apartment I can use," she said, with all the firmness her decidedly weak voice could muster. She wished that somehow he would stop searching her face with those eyes—why did they have to look at her so . . . in a way that wound around her heart, casting a special spell all its own?

"Why?" she asked at last. "Why do you want me to stay on the ranch?" She sighed long and sat up higher. "Look," she began, feeling suddenly able to face the situation square on. "I don't want to go back to Casa Contenta. I've already told you what I want. And now I realize that, since you don't care—I mean I understand what you want, but it just isn't what I want."

His eyes had turned a deep emerald and remained filled with that certain compelling light that bypassed all rational thought. Then he smiled. "I think, Jennifer, that you're a fool, as big a fool as I am—no, don't interrupt me," he said, motioning her to keep quiet and moving to hitch one hip on the edge of the bed, where he eased himself down to a sitting position.

He was suddenly so close, and while one part of her ached to reach out and caress his tanned cheek, the other part dared not.

"It seems the entire time we've known each other we've both been missing the point."

"And what is the point?" she asked. "What are you saying?"

He took her so much smaller hand in his and stroked the back of her knuckles. "I want you to stay on the ranch, Jennifer, and not just to train horses, but to be with me. I want you . . . I want to make you happy. Haven't you ever realized that was what I wanted?"

She didn't have a chance to say no as he continued. "You are the only woman I've ever really wanted." He pulled her to a sitting position, into the warmth and strength of his arms. "Don't you see what I'm trying to tell you?" And when she only shook her head, her eyes wide, afraid to put into words what the miraculous lifting of her heart told her, he leaned closer and said, "I love you."

Jennifer stared. So simple, three words—and yet they seemed to change everything. And it was as if her heart opened, even as it skipped a beat before racing faster, and from it she uttered his name—"Flint," soft and full of her own surging emotions. She squeezed his hand tighter, a small frown between her brows, half expecting a denial as

182

she watched his face. But he remained looking at her as the knowledge sank in.

"But why didn't you tell me?" she asked at last. "Why did you let me think . . ."

"Why?" His eyebrows raised incredulously. "Do you have any idea how aloof you've been? You're as skittish as that filly of yours. Just when I thought I was making progress, everything would fall apart. I thought that experiencing our love physically would make a difference, but afterward you were as cold as ever. I was afraid if I told you how I felt you would bolt."

It seemed impossible, yet he was holding her, telling her things she had hardly dared to hope. She looked up at him, making no effort to hide her feelings now, knowing her eyes were full of love and now a hint of amusement as she considered this big man admitting that he was afraid of anything.

His usually commanding jaw had softened until he suddenly seemed more vulnerable than she had ever imagined. "But now I've told you," he continued, "and I'm going to take care of you, Jennifer, for the next week, no matter what you say. After that, if you still want to leave, then you'll be free to go."

The joy in her bubbled over into a laugh. "We've both been fools," she said. "When I finally realized I wanted you, I was just angry because you knew it and worried you would use it against me. And I was angry when you guessed so much about my past."

"Do you think you'll ever tell me about it?" he asked, running the back of his fingers along the line of her jaw, then pushing back her hair.

"Sometime. It doesn't seem so important anymore," she said, realizing that the memory of Dirk now had a vague distant sense of something that had happened very long ago.

He squeezed her close, yet with infinite gentleness. "Then we'll consider this a beginning," he said firmly.

"A beginning?"

"Yes, our beginning. We're going to spend our life together sharing our dreams and ourselves, a life of building, among other things, the finest Arabian ranch in the country, if that's what you want."

She nodded. "Yes, the finest."

His eyes shone. "Next year we'll raise a new barn and plant the fields gold with hay, and we'll breed every mare until by spring we'll have pastures full of beautiful long-legged foals. Now that we're together, we're going to make Casa Contenta really content for the first time."

Jennifer felt a bursting warmth inside her as she went into his arms. "Yes, yes, oh, yes," she said, squeezing him tight until her leg throbbed painfully and she leaned to rub it.

"But all this 'beginning' is going to have to wait until next week while I stay in bed," she said. "Doctor's orders, you remember."

He regarded her with twinkling eyes, leaning her back so she lay across his lap, his lips poised over hers. "Our beginning won't have to wait. I can think of wonderful ways to 'begin' without your ever getting out of bed. Haven't I told you"—he leaned to kiss her nose—"I'm a good improviser."

As he kissed her Jennifer felt all doubts and thoughts of the past being swept away before the tenderness in that caress and suddenly, smiling inwardly, Jennifer considered that their first week of "beginning" was not going to seem nearly long enough.

# Desert Hostage

## Diane Dunaway

Behind her is England and her first innocent encounter with love. Before her is a mysterious land of forbidding majesty. Kidnapped, swept across the deserts of Araby, Juliette Barclay sees her past vanish in the endless, shifting sands. Desperate and defiant, she seeks escape only to find harrowing danger, to discover her one hope in the arms of her captor, the Shiek of El Abadan. Fearless and proud, he alone can tame her. She alone can possess his soul. Between them lies the secret that will bind her to him forever, a woman possessed, a slave of love.

**A DELL BOOK**          11963-4    $3.95

# Seize The Dawn

## by Vanessa Royall

For as long as she could remember, Elizabeth Rolfson knew that her destiny lay in America. She arrived in Chicago in 1885, the stunning heiress to a vast empire. As men of daring pressed westward, vying for the land, Elizabeth was swept into the savage struggle. Driven to learn the secret of her past, to find the one man who could still the restlessness of her heart, she would stand alone against the mighty to claim her proud birthright and grasp a dream of undying love.

A DELL BOOK    17788-X    $3.50

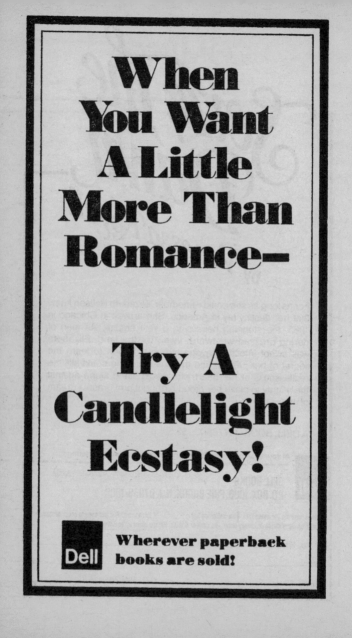

# COMING
# IN
# AUGUST—

# NEW DELL

**TEMPESTUOUS EDEN,**
by Heather Graham.
$2.50

Blair Morgan—daughter of a powerful man, widow of a famous senator—sacrifices a world of wealth to work among the needy in the Central American jungle and meets Craig Taylor, a man she can deny nothing.

**EMERALD FIRE,**
by Barbara Andrews
$2.50

She was stranded on a deserted island with a handsome millionaire—what more could Kelly want? Love.

# NEW DELL

### CANDLELIGHT
## Ecstasy Supreme

## LOVERS AND PRETENDERS,
### by Prudence Martin
### $2.50

Christine and Paul—looking for new lives on a cross-country jaunt, were bound by lies and a passion that grew more dangerously honest with each passing day. Would the truth destroy their love?

## WARMED BY THE FIRE,
### by Donna Kimel Vitek
### $2.50

When malicious gossip forces Juliet to switch jobs from one television network to another, she swears an office romance will never threaten her career again—until she meets superstar anchorman Marc Tyner.

# Dell | **Bestsellers**

- [ ] **QUINN** by Sally Mandel .............................**$3.50** (17176-8)
- [ ] **STILL THE MIGHTY WATERS**
  by Janice Young Brooks ...........................**$3.95** (17630-1)
- [ ] **NORTH AND SOUTH** by John Jakes .......**$4.95** (16204-1)
- [ ] **THE SEEDS OF SINGING**
  by Kay McGrath ........................................**$3.95** (19120-3)
- [ ] **GO SLOWLY, COME BACK QUICKLY**
  by David Niven...........................................**$3.95** (13113-8)
- [ ] **SEIZE THE DAWN** by Vanessa Royal .......**$3.50** (17788-X)
- [ ] **PALOMINO** by Danielle Steel ....................**$3.50** (16753-1)
- [ ] **BETTE: THE LIFE OF BETTE DAVIS**
  by Charles Higham .....................................**$3.95** (10662-1)